Coffin in Malta

Olive laboured up the steps with frequent pants for breath, her heart was bad tonight. She was almost at her door when, through the quiet night, she heard the noises begin.

John Azzopardi, lying quietly asleep, was awakened by the sound of a woman wailing. It was a loud strong sound, not a scream or a cry but the sort of sound that the Trojan women might have made. It might have been the voice of Electra.

He stumbled to the window and looked down the street. In the light streaming through the open door behind her he saw silhouetted a woman he recognised as Amelia Grech. She was standing there, letting a tremendous cry of despair and outrage well out of her great wide mouth, and holding forward on her outstretched arms a human head.

She looked like Salome with the head of John the Baptist.

The voice of Electra and the appearance of Salome carrying the head of the Baptist.

Other titles in the Walker British Mystery Series

Peter Alding • MURDER IS SUSPECTED
Peter Alding • RANSOM TOWN
Jeffrey Ashford • SLOW DOWN THE WORLD
Jeffrey Ashford • THREE LAYERS OF GUILT
Pierre Audemars • NOW DEAD IS ANY MAN
Marion Babson • DANGEROUS TO KNOW
Marion Babson • THE LORD MAYOR OF DEATH
Brian Ball • MONTENEGRIN GOLD
Josephine Bell • A QUESTION OF INHERITANCE
Josephine Bell • TREACHERY IN TYPE
Josephine Bell • VICTIM
W. J. Burley • DEATH IN WILLOW PATTERN
W. J. Burley • TO KILL A CAT
Desmond Cory • THE NIGHT HAWK
Desmond Cory • UNDERTOW
John Creasey • THE BARON AND THE UNFINISHED PORTRAIT
John Creasey • HELP FROM THE BARON
John Creasey • THE TOFF AND THE FALLEN ANGELS
John Creasey • TRAP THE BARON
June Drummond • FUNERAL URN
June Drummond • SLOWLY THE POISON
William Haggard • THE NOTCH ON THE KNIFE
William Haggard • THE POISON PEOPLE
William Haggard • TOO MANY ENEMIES
William Haggard • VISA TO LIMBO
William Haggard • YESTERDAY'S ENEMY
Simon Harvester • MOSCOW ROAD
Simon Harvester • ZION ROAD
J. G. Jeffreys • SUICIDE MOST FOUL
J. G. Jeffreys • A WICKED WAY TO DIE
J. G. Jeffreys • THE WILFUL LADY
Elizabeth Lemarchand • CHANGE FOR THE WORSE
Elizabeth Lemarchand • STEP IN THE DARK
Elizabeth Lemarchand • SUDDENLY WHILE GARDENING
Elizabeth Lemarchand • UNHAPPY RETURNS
Laurie Mantell • A MURDER OR THREE
John Sladek • BLACK AURA
John Sladek • INVISIBLE GREEN

GWENDOLINE BUTLER
Coffin in Malta

WALKER AND COMPANY · NEW YORK

Copyright © 1964 by Gwendoline Butler

All rights reserved. No part of this book may be reproduced or transmitted in any form or by any means, electric or mechanical, including photocopying, recording, or by any information storage and retrieval system, without permission in writing from the Publisher.

All the characters and events portrayed in this story are fictitious.

First published in the United States of America in 1965 by the Walker Publishing Company, Inc.

This paperback edition first published in 1985.

ISBN: 0-8027-3111-2

Library of Congress Catalog Card Number: 65-23264

Printed in the United States of America.

10 9 8 7 6 5 4 3 2 1

LIST OF CHARACTERS

John Azzopardi
Dr. Joseph De Bono
Sergeant Alfred Grima
The Baroness Lily Louise Castaldi
Chloe Zarb
Alice De Bono
Amelia Grech and her husband, Carmel Grech (cousin of her deceased first husband, Nazareno Grech)
Hector Grech
Rose Grech
Peter and Violet Fenech
Mary and Phyllis Colombo
Mr. and Mrs. Axisa
Mrs Callus
Inspector John Coffin from London

Before the Inquisition

I

"The winter smell of Malta is the smell of kerosene," thought John Azzopardi, as he came from the airport to Vallctta. He had left behind him a London shrouded in fog and frost and come to this golden world with sunlight striking off the amber stone of the austere palaces and fortifications of the Knights of St. John. The road from the airport curved down through the stony yellow countryside, passed the racecourse and through the suburb of factories of Marsa, and then wound upwards through the great stone walls and gates of Floriana, built to defend Europe against the Turks. Everywhere was bright and open.

The car climbed the majestic balustraded slope of the flyover into Valletta, and ran into the square by the Auberge de Castile and came to a halt.

John got out of the car and stood there in the sunlight, smiling. Castile was empty of people but a few cars were parked over one corner by the Upper Barracca Gardens, where children were playing. It looked friendly and peaceful and to John Azzopardi it looked very much like home. He remembered the conversation in the plane with the stewardess who had discovered he was a lawyer.

"I shouldn't think there's much crime in Malta."

"You can have litigation without crime. But no, there's no serious crime in Malta."

It was winter, however, and it could be chilly and was often damp even in the Mediterranean, and the houses all over the steep, stepped streets of the old city of Valletta were heated with kerosene stoves. "Paraffin, back in London," he thought, for he was still poised uneasily in the spirit between London, where he had been living for three years, and Malta, where he had been born. "Paraffin, kerosene, it's all the same stuff."

But it was the smell of kerosene in which the smell of new baked bread, the orange harvest, and the scent of incense floating out of the church all mingled.

He paid off the taxi and humped his bags down the stone staircase which was the street to his flat. It had stood empty for three years but he knew it would be clean and polished and ready for him because his aunt the Baroness Castaldi had assured him she would see to it. He was one of a family of seven and his mother had had six sisters, so there was always an aunt or a sister to help out when needed.

He climbed up the three flights of stairs to his flat, found his key and opened the door, remembering automatically, even after a three years' gap, that you had to press on the key as you turned it. The flat was empty, as he had expected, and highly polished. Obviously Aunt Lily Louise had found a good maid, for she had not done the work herself with her long well-diamonded fingers. She had left a bunch of flowers and a batch of savoury cheese tartlets, made according to her own recipe, on the table. She had also left behind her own particular scent of sandalwood and jasmine mixed. An envelope addressed to him, in her round flowing writing, rested against the dish of tarts. Aunt Lily Louise was far and away the most worldly and decorative, as well as the most efficient, of his aunts. He groped in his pocket where rested the bottle of French scent he had bought for her, and felt, as he had done when he was a child, the familiar twinge of anxiety whether she would like her present. If she didn't, she would say so.

He went to the window and drew back the curtains, which had been drawn, according to the Maltese fashion, against the midday sun, but after three years in London he felt he wanted to see the sun. The Grand Harbour lay beneath him, elegant, spacious and almost empty. The day of the great fleets was over. Two destroyers flying the White Ensign and a tanker from Holland floated there in emptiness.

The sun flooded into the room and he could see that Aunt Lily Louise had indeed done her work well; not a speck of dust anywhere, and everything shone. There was no carpet on the black and red tiled floor, only a rug or two placed by the desk and by the sofa. To eyes still used to his London flat it looked a little bare. He remembered that he did have a carpet, but it was not yet December, and no carpets were laid on floors in Malta before December and sometimes not until the New Year. But

Aunt Lily Louise had hung up his winter curtains, no doubt thinking it wouldn't be worth putting up the thin summer muslins just for a few weeks.

"I like it all," he thought, looking around him and out of the window. "All of it."

His law books had been given a prominent position on the shelves. Aunt Lily Louise again. She approved of him as a lawyer. His grandfather had been a judge, his father had followed him, and he reckoned that at least four of his cousins were now barristers in Valletta. It was quite a little circle he had come back to. And he had come back.

But the trouble with coming back was: did you ever come back the same? Time alone would show.

A mosquito from the well in the garden down below buzzed around the room and over his head. He slapped it back. He had forgotten about the well and the mosquitoes, probably he had forgotten about lots of other things too.

Across the road the bell sounded in the parish church for evening service. The bell made a tinny hard little clang, very familiar to him and not unpleasing. He leaned out of his window to listen. He could hear bells ringing out over the city, the noise of traffic, and floating upwards the sounds of shouts and laughter. It was now dark, the sun having set suddenly and completely, without the twilight to which he had grown used, but there were lights studding the darkness everywhere, and as he looked he saw a shower of coloured sparks from a firework display fly upwards. Some little town somewhere across the harbour was having a festa to celebrate its saint. As he stood there he heard a loud conversation start up in the house across the narrow street. He couldn't pick out the words but the voices sounded angry. They may not have been; his ears were out of tune for the cadences of his home town, and his neighbours may merely have started up an animated conversation.

He laughed, sat down, and took Aunt Lily Louise Castaldi's letter.

Inside the envelope was a note and an invitation. The invitation, engraved in gold on a large folded sheet of thick paper, was to a wedding. The wedding to be solemnised was between Giorgio Zarb and Mary Trentullo. He raised his eyebrows: his cousin George, married at last, and to the little Trentullo girl. He noticed the Italianisation of his cousin's name on the invitation and wondered what that meant? George had been George all the days he had known him. He seemed to remember that the Trentullos had an Italian grandmother, but that couldn't affect George, surely?

He replaced the invitation in the envelope and took up his aunt's letter.

"My dear nephew," it began. "It is my pleasure to welcome you back. You should find all your flat in good order. Your tenants took good care of it while you were away. He was a naval officer and they have now gone back to England. They broke two plates but have replaced them. The pink glass from Murano they could not, unhappily, replace, but they have left you that charming plaque of Our Lady, which I chose for them to make up for it."

He looked thoughtful: one of Aunt Lily Louise's plaques. Aunt Lily Louise's plaques were famous, and not only throughout her family. Amongst her many other projects she ran a small ceramics factory to help unemployment. Her workers made plates, plaques, small figures and pots and bowls. Some of them were charming, others less so. It all depended who had charge of the designing at the time, and this in turn depended on numerous factors too chancey to reckon on, such as who was away sick, whose daughter was getting married and so needed more pay, and how Aunt Lily Louise's rheumatism was anyway. She had a tall, slim, elegant spine which gave her hell in the damp weather. When it was bad her tongue was sharp so that the design and output of her factory was often related to the toll her temper was taking on her designers. Sometimes she did the design and that was fatal. Always chic and well turned out herself, when she got near a blank ceramic surface all sense of balance and harmony deserted her, and although she painted her own face beautifully she couldn't get paint on the plates with the same dexterity.

He looked round the room and saw a plaque suspended above the radio. He had got one of Aunt Lily Louise's own special plaques. He grinned; it had probably been on sale all the year and failed to find a buyer. Aunt Lily Louise, who had been called Zarb, was from Gozo, the neighbouring island, and among the Maltese the Gozitans enjoy the respect accorded the Scots in England.

The letter went on: "I hope you will come to lunch

here with me on Tuesday, at twelve, punctually, if you please."

Lunch at the Palazzo Castaldi had always been a treat when he was younger; it was still, but it was typical of his aunt that she left him no choice anyway. It was a royal command. Typical also was the early hour, which was set so that his aunt's old cook Carità and her even older sister, Stella, who was housemaid, could depart for an afternoon's visit to their family in the country near St. Paul's Bay. John knew that neither of the old women cared much for visiting their family, with whom they quarrelled, but dutifully departed each week because Aunt Lily Louise had decreed that *naturally* they wished to see their nephews and nieces. (They had much outlived their younger but married sisters and brothers.)

He put the letter in his pocket and rose to look out of the window. He could see straight down over his little iron balcony to the street below. It was a street made in the form of a great, shallow, stone staircase. He looked at it with pleasure because he was home. He had finished his work in London, had made a success of it and had tempting offers to stay there, but he had come home.

"I was right to come back, though," he thought. "Everyone who lives on an island should always go back to that island." And he smiled.

From the window he saw the figure of a boy come stumbling awkwardly down the steps. The boy had a large red face with fine round brown eyes and a mane of dark hair. His body was round and plump, like a bolster case, and his arms and legs were short and thick like pillows. On his face was a fixed intent stare and he was making little hooting noises through his mouth as he ran. He carried a tin whistle in one hand, a stick in the other. Although awkward, he was agile enough and hopped from step to step like a goat.

John stared at him; the boy was a very familiar figure, although, until now, a forgotten one. He was a well-known local character, Hector Grech, the simple son of Amelia Grech, who was a laundress living across the way. He started to remember Amelia.

As he watched, he saw Amelia Grech, wearing an apron and an old hat, appear on the steps higher up and shout to her son. A man walked out from a doorway behind her and stood watching; he was smiling.

The boy Hector stopped, picked up the cat he had been chasing and went obediently back up the steps to his mother. He was shaking his head from side to side, as if worried, as he climbed. He had come down quickly; he went back slowly.

"They don't look as if they're caring for the boy too well," thought John Azzopardi, observing the stained and torn clothes, the uncut hair and dirty face.

The church bells had stopped ringing, the little group on the steps disappeared into the house and the black cat fled back down the steps and sat washing its face in a doorway.

John drew his curtains and went back into his warm, lighted room.

The Inquisitor offered a cigarette to the policeman

who was visiting him and took one himself. "Inquisitor" was the nickname the Valletta police gave to him; it wasn't his official title, which was that of Officiating Magistrate. He was the lawyer appointed to attend as the police questioned witnesses and suspects in a criminal investigation; he also might take statements and ask questions. His other name was Dr. Joseph De Bono.

"Yes, it was a bad case," he said, "that bank murder affair, but an interesting one all the same."

"Too interesting for me," said the policeman, lighting his cigarette. "I like a quiet life." He was Sergeant Grima.

"Oh well, we hardly ever get a murder, do we? And when we do, in a closely-knit community like we are, it's usually no secret, is it?"

"He can't help putting everything in the interrogative," thought the policeman. "Even sitting here, just having a quiet smoke, he's still asking me questions."

"No," he said aloud. "I mean yes." He frowned at his colleague, whom he suspected, and quite rightly, of being cleverer than he was. "All the same, people can keep secrets. I had a man in the other day, and he managed to keep it a secret from his employer for twenty years that he had a wife and another job over in Gozo."

"He must have worked for an Englishman," said the Inquisitor in a level voice and without a smile.

He lived in a tall, narrow old house which had been the home of the Ministry of Rations during the war. He had his offices on the lower floor and kept his family on the top two floors. It was a medieval arrangement but comfortable and meant that he could enjoy his wife's cooking for lunch.

"Well, you can't make an arrest yet in this case of suspected arson in Kingsway, you don't have enough evidence."

"What a shame. I'd like to make an arrest before Christmas," said the policeman wistfully.

"You're lazy. Go back and see the garage owner again... All that petrol."

"Very well. Yes, that's a good idea," he said, his enthusiasm brightening. "He's an honest man himself, though... He's my cousin."

"But not all his employees are honest, perhaps."

"No. True."

"Well, that's it, then." The Inquisitor stood up; the interview, half formal, half friendly, conducted in the manner he had developed so well, was over. Besides, he could smell the fragrance of his wife's soup floating down from above.

The policeman stood up too and they shook hands.

"I'm expecting my cousin John Azzopardi back today from London," said the Inquisitor. "You remember him?"

"Really?" said the policeman; he was interested. "Now there *is* a man who can keep a secret."

"Yes," agreed the Inquisitor and they both stood for a second reflecting on the secret which John Azzopardi had kept for three years and was still successfully keeping.

The sun made golden the stone of the Castaldi Palace

which was now in its fourth century. Not old, perhaps, as buildings go, but old as a lived-in family home. It was nothing out of the way architecturally and was flanked on either side with other houses just as old and more beautiful; but only the Castaldi Palace had remained continually in the hands of one family. The Castaldis were a tough and energetic, if not very handsome clan. They had been rich four centuries ago and they were rich now, although they took care not to mention it too much. Frederick Castaldi had been well able to afford to marry handsome, poor Lily Louise Zarb, one of the family of beautiful daughters of a Gozo judge. "And look how well it worked for him," people said later, pointing to the great success of Lily Louise in loving, ruling and finally surviving her husband.

The sound of chickens clucking and hooting floated over the terrace as John Azzopardi walked across the garden to greet his aunt. He could see Aunt Lily Louise and the cook Carità in the hen-run, their heads bent in conversation. They seemed to have a nun with them.

This did not surprise John Azzopardi, who knew that his aunt would have a cardinal into the hen-run if that was where her walk happened to lead her. And as a matter of fact, her hens were something special. They were aristocrats among hens, with bright wicked eyes and shrill voices. They made extraordinary tough eating but were splendid layers of eggs.

"Chicken for lunch today," said his aunt by way of greeting.

"It's always chicken for lunch today," said John, bowing slightly towards his aunt and the nun.

Carità tittered; she had killed the hen, cooked it and knew all about its constitution, muscles and sinews, all of which had been excellent.

"And this is Mother Mary Anthony," said Aunt Lily Louise. "She is the senior history mistress at St. Bonaventura's."

Mother Mary Anthony smiled politely, then turned back to the Baroness and said briskly: "Now, about the girl, you'll take her then? She's a nice, kind, intelligent girl and will make an excellent secretary."

"I don't really want a secretary."

"You want this one; she'll look after the hens beautifully." She cast her eyes round at the shrieking birds. "And possibly get you off hens and on to a more worthwhile hobby. She knows a lot about pictures. You could get interested in pictures."

"I'm not interested in pictures."

"They'd make a good hobby."

"Not so profitable as my hens."

"You can't tell. So that's settled." She began to walk out of the hen-run. A small scurry of birds fluttered above and around her so that she looked a rather fiercer St. Francis.

"Well, I don't know," began the Baroness Castaldi. "I'm very comfortable as I am."

Mother Mary Anthony turned to face her hostess. "It's your *duty* to take the girl. She must be got out of the house where she is now. She might *marry* this boy."

Carità muttered something.

"Oh well, if it's a question of mortal sin," began Aunt Lily Louise.

"Mortal sin, mortal sin," said Mother Mary Anthony explosively. "That's just like you, always going on about mortal sin. A situation can be just as difficult and tiresome, let me tell you, without being mortal sin . . . There's no mortal sin about this girl. She wouldn't misbehave, poor little rabbit."

"First chickens, now rabbits," observed John Azzopardi mildly, making his first independent remark.

Mother Mary Anthony looked at him, gave a laugh, and then walked quickly up the path, her gown floating behind her. The others followed her more slowly, the Baroness talking and John quietly enjoying the sun on his back.

"I can see you always accept what she says," he remarked.

"Very nearly always," agreed his aunt. "Not quite always. No one could."

They ate in the impressive dining-room hung with gilt framed portraits of Castaldis in eighteenth- and nineteenth-century dress. They were a prosperous but ill-favoured lot, all the good looks for which her offspring were now famous had come into the family with Lily Louise Zarb. By a miracle of genetics big, oval, brown eyes had triumphed over small, bad, black, beady ones, long, graceful bones over short, thick ones and a shining delicacy of skin over one distinctly swarthy. But all Aunt Lily Louise's beautiful boys and girls were now scattered, a girl in Washington married to a diplomat, a boy in India working for U.N.O., two girls married in France and Italy, and a fourth, the gayest and most sociable of all, had entered an enclosed Order two years ago.

A soft breeze blew into the room over the cyclamen and verbena that flowered there in pots on the window sill.

"We shall have a good orange harvest this year," said his aunt as they chewed their chicken.

"Can I have some?" The Castaldi oranges were famous. They were watered from a well in the garden and were said to have a special flavour on this account.

"You shall have a box."

"I've cracked a tooth, I think."

"Cracked a tooth? You can't have. Not on Grizelda, she was always one of the tenderest of my birds."

"And how long did Grizelda enjoy this pre-eminence?" said John Azzopardi, rubbing his cheek.

"Two or three years, I think."

"That explains it." He drank a long draught of Gozo wine to soothe him; it was excellent wine, amber, clear and the colour of the landscape itself in sunlight.

After lunch they sat on the flagged terrace and drank the salty, strange coffee of Valetta.

"They say the water is better up at Mdina," said Aunt Lily Louise. "But I always think my water is best." She finished her drink complacently.

John Azzopardi drank his more slowly; it was going to take him some time to get used to the flavour again after three years away from it. He sipped it cautiously once more: it looked like coffee but it tasted like brine.

He put down his cup with a small sigh. Give him a day or two and he wouldn't notice. For a moment he was far away, on another island, grey and smoke shrouded, and a voice was saying: "With my love, John, but good-bye," and he could taste the coffee hot and strong in his mouth. "No one should say good-bye over a cup of coffee," he thought. "It's the wrong drink."

He turned to his aunt.

"Come on, let's have all the news," he commanded. "Out with it."

"You may have been abroad. You haven't been out of touch," she protested. "We've all written letters."

"There's plenty of news you wouldn't put in letters."

"True." She smiled.

John looked across the terrace towards the statue of the boy which stood near the famous well. There was nothing much else to be seen, for winter is winter even in the Mediterranean.

"How's Chloe?"

At the sound of the question Aunt Lily Louise's delicate lips tightened; she did not answer.

"What? Do you women still hate Chloe? You were all raising your eyebrows and looking censorious three years ago when I left. Time stands still here."

"My dear, Chloe herself has hardly stood still since you left us . . . Oh, we don't know that she is actually unfaithful to Bertie."

"And would you blame her if she was? He lost all her

money, killed the child and spent all his time soaking in the Phoenicia bar."

"He does drink. I admit that he drinks." Aunt Lily Louise's eyebrows rose in a frown. She sighed. "He is more like an Englishman in that." The Maltese do not drink: it is not one of their vices.

"There you are then."

"All the same . . . So many admirers . . . You know they joke about Chloe's Chorus?"

John was silent: he was bitterly angry at the cruelty of the joke. His aunt did not notice this; the truth was that she was not an especially sensitive woman.

"The trouble with Chloe," she said reflectively, "is that she is always such an open, talkative sort of person."

"You blame her for that? Is that a fault?"

"It can be, I'm afraid," said his aunt, rather coldly. "It very often is in a woman, especially one placed in a position like Chloe's."

The wind seemed to have been getting stronger since they sat down.

"The wind seems colder, there is rain in it." His aunt shivered: she got up. "I hope it isn't going to turn into a gregale. Let's go in.

"And what are you going to do now you are back, nephew?"

"I shall work hard and make a career for myself."

"Nothing else?" She was studying his face.

"I hadn't thought about anything else," he admitted.

"Some men do remain bachelors," she said placidly. "I approve of that."

John Azzopardi smiled wryly. You cut yourself in two (for reasons that seemed good to you, although they had not seemed so to your English friends), and your Aunt Lily Louise simply smiled and said some men did remain bachelors.

"Your cousin Joseph De Bono is very interested in your arrival," said his aunt.

"He was very interested in my departure."

Aunt Lily Louise laughed. "I think he was always a little jealous that it was to *you* that," she hesitated for a word, "the confession was made. You could call it a confession, I suppose?"

"I have never done so," said John Azzopardi carefully, and in the circumstances, obstinately. "And he's not really my cousin," he added irritably. "A distant relation, that's all."

His aunt sighed. "England has affected you more than you know."

John Azzopardi drove himself back to his flat alone through the rays of the afternoon sun. Very soon now it would be dark. He had enjoyed his day, but with it had come the uncomfortable feeling that at least two of the problems he had left behind him when he departed three years ago were still here waiting for him.

The lights were beginning to shine out everywhere in Valletta when he parked his car in Castile Square at the top of his street and went quickly down the steps to his front door.

The door was open and the light was on in the

hallway. But no one was there. Or so he thought at first. Then he saw that there was someone crouching under the stairs. He leaned forward and looked.

"What's the matter there?" he said gently. He could sense the fear.

It was the young maid, Mary Colombo, who cleaned his flat and the two other flats in the building; she worked here with her older sister. She looked at him now out of a grubby dishevelled face, big brown eyes staring. She had almost certainly been crying.

"Are you ill?" he asked. He remembered the Baroness telling him there was measles among the families in St. Michael's Street.

"I was just resting here, out of the way," she said.

"Out of the way? But what a place to do it!"

"I'm just resting here till my sister comes to take me home."

"But where do you live? Is it so far?"

"St. Michael's Street," she said reluctantly. She was already getting up and getting herself ready to depart.

"But that's just the next street." He was surprised. "Are you frightened to go that distance?"

She didn't answer.

"And you left the door open, too," he said, still puzzled.

"No, I didn't," she said quickly. "That wasn't me..."

"Someone did."

She hurried to the door and looked up and down the street.

"What are you looking for?" asked John Azzopardi, watching her face.

"I can go now," she said, not turning her head towards him, "without waiting for my sister."

She darted out of the door, up the steps and round the corner into St. Michael's Street out of sight.

John Azzopardi stood there watching. As he watched he saw a family group, mother and son, appear at the bottom and slowly start the ascent of the street. One was the boy, Hector Grech, he had seen staggering down the street on the day he arrived, and on the other side of the boy, with her hand on his shoulder was Amelia Grech, aged forty-three, washerwoman of Valletta. They came slowly up the steps, the woman walking heavily and slightly retarding the progress of the pair. She carried her big, almost masculine figure proudly. She had a curious way of swinging her right arm as if clearing a path for herself and her son.

Perhaps in a way she had been doing just that all her life, thought John Azzopardi, clearing a way for herself and her son.

Slowly he closed the door and went back into the hall, the scene of his late encounter with the girl. A faint, sour, sweet smell that he was unable to identify hung over the hall, joining with, but not defeating the smell of kerosene. Long afterwards he thought that what he had smelt then was the smell of fear.

That night Amelia Grech worked late and hard; she did her washing in the old-fashioned way with tub and boiler and bleach. Her big, muscular arms moved tirelessly, scrubbing and wringing and rinsing till she was satisfied with the whiteness of her sheets.

She hung up the big coarse sheets and the thick towels on the line in the kitchen, then she cleaned out the big boiler and opened the windows to let out some of the steam.

She went into the bedroom next door where her girls lay and looked at them closely but they were sound asleep; then she went into the room where the boy Hector slept, and finally she went back into the living-room and sat down. She was used to working in a hot steamy atmosphere but this work tonight had made her thirsty.

It was about nine-thirty and although late for doing the laundry, it was not late for going out to seek some society.

"I'll go round to Harry's Bar," she muttered to herself, rubbing the back of her hand across the mouth, "and see Olive and we'll have a talk." – Olive Feltcher was her friend, who worked in Harry's Bar. "It's time I had a talk with Olive."

She put on her coat, lowered the light in the room where she had been sitting and went quietly out into the street.

Amelia and her family lived on the ground floor of a large house in which each floor was let out to different families. Almost everyone was in bed except Amelia, for most of her neighbours got up very early and were at work before six. Amelia and her friend Olive got up early too but they stayed up late as well.

Awake also and still crying miserably was the little

maid Mary whom John Azzopardi had seen that night in tears already. She and her sister lived in this house too. Now she gripped her hands together tightly and tried to stop crying.

Amelia looked up at the tall, dark, shuttered house and thought of all the Fenechs and Colombos sleeping peacefully there. She thought also of her own family asleep.

"But who could hurt those sleeping innocents?" she said to herself and hurried out to drink red wine and laugh with Olive in Harry's Bar down by the harbour.

"You advertise red wine but what you've really got is vinegar," said Amelia to Olive, after about four glasses of it.

Harry's Bar was still open, it remained opened as long as Olive chose for it to remain open, but there were no customers except Amelia, and she didn't pay.

"We had a sailor in tonight," said Olive. "First one this week. Once, hundreds."

Both she and Amelia spoke English to each other, Amelia with a strong accent but fair fluency and Olive with a faint residual Cockney whine. Olive was a languageless person, an illiterate polyglot, her English was stunted and she hardly spoke Maltese. She was the daughter of an English father and a Maltese mother.

"You and your sailors," said Amelia.

"Well," said Olive bridling. She was a tiny woman beside Amelia Grech's sturdy and massive figure.

"Give me another drink."

"No, you've had four. Free."

Amelia reached out and took the bottle. "Wine as

rotten as this ought to be free," she said contemptuously. The bottle rolled from the table and a little wine trickled onto the sawdust-covered floor. Olive scuttled after it, muttering; she was both mean and scrupulously clean.

"Drunk," she called over her shoulder at Amelia; they always ended up by quarrelling.

"Dirty," called Amelia back. Olive accepted the insult, although she resented it.

Amelia stood up. She looked a fine, even a noble figure as she walked to the door.

"Wait for me," said Olive, hastily drawing the shutters and locking up. "I'm coming too."

They walked up the steps from the harbour together, parting at the bottom of St. Michael's Street, Amelia to go up it and Olive to hurry along, past the Church of St. Michael to the Street of the Gold-workers.

Olive stood for a while watching her friend make her slow regal ascent to her home. Then she turned; on her own she looked what she was, a quiet, impaired, respectable woman. It was only when in company with Amelia that she seemed a little raffish – their relationship accentuated strange qualities in both of them.

Olive laboured up the steps with frequent pants for breath, her heart was bad tonight. She was almost at her door when, through the quiet night, she heard the noises begin.

John Azzopardi, lying quietly asleep, was awakened by the sound of a woman wailing. It was a loud strong sound, not a scream or a cry but the sort of sound that the Trojan women might have made. It might have been the voice of Electra.

He stumbled to the window and looked down the street. In the light streaming through the open door behind her he saw silhouetted a woman he recognised as Amelia Grech. She was standing there, letting a tremendous cry of despair and outrage well out of her great wide mouth, and holding forward on her outstretched arms a human head.

She looked like Salome with the head of John the Baptist.

The voice of Electra and the appearance of Salome carrying the head of the Baptist.

II

John Azzopardi was not the first person to reach Amelia Grech. By the time he got there some of her neighbours had appeared, but he was the first to take control.

Amelia Grech was still standing there with her terrible burden, but she was silent now. Her head was raised and she was staring straight forward. Blood had stained the front of her coat and dripped on to her shoes.

Three women and two men were standing in a group staring at her. They were motionless and quite dumb.

"Why don't they move or speak," thought John Azzopardi, "instead of just standing there?"

As he approached, first one and then another turned and, still silent, went back into the house. One old woman lingered, peering from the stairs, then she too disappeared.

John Azzopardi limped up, having banged his foot on the granite stairs on the way up. As she saw him, and it seemed to him that her eyes focused on him with difficulty, Amelia Grech slowly walked back towards the door of the house, stopped, and placed her burden on the steps. Then she positioned herself straight and erect beside it like a sentry.

She waited until John got right up to her, then she spoke.

"You see what they have done to me?" She stared at him in the face and said again, "You see what they have done to me?" She spoke in a harsh voice but without emphasis, as if what she said was a self-evident truth.

He took her by the arm and tried to lead her into the house but she resisted him; she was as firm and immovable as a rock.

Suddenly she opened her mouth and cried out again like an animal. The noise of her wailing echoed and re-echoed round the steep street of narrow, tall houses.

No one came out, no one appeared. John Azzopardi was aware that people stood silently behind shutters and curtains but not one person appeared in the street.

Suddenly he heard the sound of running and a policeman became visible at the top of the steps. He halted as he saw them, stood quite still for a second taking in what he saw, and then slowly descended the steps towards them.

He crossed himself hurriedly as he saw the head lying there with staring eyes and John Azzopardi somewhat belatedly did the same. If there was a restoration or offering of respect or dignity possible to that poor riven creature whose head lay before them, then he wanted to contribute.

The policeman knelt down to study the head now and for the first time John Azzopardi really saw it. A thatch of unbrushed hair fell around the features, obscuring them until the hair was brushed aside. The face itself was empty with vacant eyes and loose mouth; the skin, however, was dirty and stained with blood; what looked like a purple bruise was showing along one cheek. It could have been some post-mortem change or it could have been a bruise made before death. The head had been severed from the trunk just below the chin.

Without surprise, without emotion, John Azzopardi performed the act of recognition.

"It's the boy Hector Grech," he said aloud. He raised his head to Amelia Grech's face. For a moment the rigid set of her features trembled, she might have burst into tears, then she controlled herself and returned his look with a blazing stare.

"She's angry," he noted with surprise. "As well as all else, as well as sorrow and misery, she feels anger," and he remembered that the great cries which she had made had been tries of outrage as well as lamentation.

"This is what they have done to me," she said again, this time speaking not impersonally as before, but directly to him.

"You'd better get into the house," he muttered.

A choking noise made him look round, and he saw the young policeman with his handkerchief to his mouth. He remembered then that he was not in company with a tough experienced London copper but a boy who had probably never seen a violent death before.

"We don't have violent crime in Malta," he found himself thinking. "This is Valletta, not London." He evoked the image of one London policeman, John Coffin, his friend, enemy, ally, accuser, for their relationship had elements of all these in it. He missed Coffin.

"Is anyone else but you coming?" he asked the boy.

"My sergeant is coming down . . . I just came ahead."

"We shall need more than your sergeant before we're through here," thought John Azzopardi grimly.

The young policeman got to his feet. He looked about eighteen and probably was little more, but he wore a wedding ring.

"He'll be bringing Dr. De Bono with him, I expect . . . you know, the Officiating Magistrate." He went over to Amelia Grech who stared at him silently. "I'll have to get you into the house, mother." Her lips tightened at this word, and he went on hastily, "Please go in and I will follow."

They stood for a moment, the policeman and the woman with the head between them, and it looked for the moment as if Amelia would not move.

"Let them all see what they have done," she said in her deep voice.

"Help me with her," he appealed to John Azzopardi. "She doesn't know what she is saying."

"I think she does." John was studying her face. "I think she does." He moved forward. "Well, if she won't, then we shall have to . . . There's only one way to do it."

He bent forward to pick up the head from her, but she was before him and she snatched up the head. Carrying her burden she stalked into the house without looking at them.

At the same moment a big car drew up at the top of the flight of steps and two men got out.

The young policeman gave a hiss of relief. "That's my boss," he said. "First time I've ever been glad to see his face." In his moment of relaxation he became loquacious. "Of course, she's a bad lot, Amelia Grech, but I wouldn't wish this on her. Not on any one... You know what it was upset me?" he said in a whisper.

John Azzopardi shook his head.

"It wasn't just seeing it... but did you notice? There were *tears* on the cheeks, it had been crying."

"Yes," said John Azzopardi, gently. "I saw that. Dried tears."

"Of course, it could perhaps have been when rain had fallen?"

"No. Tears."

Tears for what? Tears of fear? Or anger? Or love? Who could tell?

The door flapped to and fro, leading to gaping darkness beyond.

"You'd better go in after her," said John Azzopardi. "You can't tell what she'll do." – "She's capable of anything at the moment," he thought.

With an exclamation the young policeman leapt forward and disappeared through the door.

He was not too soon.

As John Azzopardi stood there a man stumbled through the door and sank down in the street at his feet. Blood was pouring from his nose.

"She kicked me out," he said. "I was only up there

trying to comfort the three girls and she kicked me out." He shook his head and the blood ran down on to his shirt. "Why should she do this to me?" He staggered to his feet. "She's a she-wolf all right . . . My wife said to me: 'Peter, you go in and talk to the girls, I can hear them calling out' . . . And this is what happens."

"You should have left it to your wife . . ." John Azzopardi looked at him.

"My wife wouldn't go in . . . Frightened. Can't you blame her? Look at me, and just for a little human kindness."

"Perhaps you should have tried it earlier," and he walked past the man, who was mopping his nose, into the house. Behind him he could hear the man talking to the police sergeant who had just arrived. "Years and years and years earlier," he added to himself.

He walked slowly into the hall, which was now brightly lit with a gas lamp, and entered the Grech flat. The young policeman stood in the middle of the room looking bewildered and three young girls, one a mere child, crouched on a battered old sofa. Amelia had disappeared into an inner room whose door stood open. The girls were crying, Amelia was wailing and the policeman was talking aloud to himself in a distracted way.

"I don't know what to do first. I ought to stop her touching things, but I can't stop her. She won't. I hope the boss comes soon. I tell you: I don't know what to do."

"I'll tell one thing you could do," said John Azzopardi, looking at the three shivering girls who hung their heads and refused to see him. "You could get coats for these three girls. They've got nothing on but their nightdresses."

"Oh yes, I'll do that, they ought to have something on for the sake of decency." And with relief at having something to do, he went into a second room which opened off the main sitting-room.

John Azzopardi looked at the three girls and saw that they were covered from neck to toe in long white nightgowns and thought they were certainly respectably covered enough for anyone. One of them, he saw, was almost certainly wearing a good many layers of clothing under her nightdress, but all three looked frightened and cold and unhappy. They were older than he had thought at first.

"Poor little beasts," he thought, but he did not speak to them; he realised that they were both timid and extremely modest. They were shy with men.

He stood there for a moment, thinking, completely unselfconsciously and genuinely unaware of the spectacle he must present in the red pyjamas he had bought at Harrod's and the tartan dressing-gown he had bought in Edinburgh, to the eyes of girls who had never been outside Valletta.

As he stood there he tried to sum up the situation. It was still only a matter of minutes, twenty at the most, although it felt like hours, since he had left his flat and come running this way, to where Amelia Grech stood with the head of her son.

He looked around. Somewhere in this flat must be the

body from which the head had been severed. The light from the room where Amelia was, caught his attention, and he saw her kneeling by the bed. He could just make out a shape upon it. He no longer had any doubts about where the trunk of Hector Grech lay.

"This is a strange murder," he thought.

He was a lawyer, but this was the first time he had been in a house where a murder had taken place. His friend, John Coffin, could have told about houses where a murder had recently taken place, about how strange they all looked with their mixture of the ordinary and the terrible – the tea in the pot and the blood on the wall, the litter of personal possessions and the body of the owner stiffening on the floor, like a Pharaoh buried among his treasures. You had to be not only tough but insensitive to be oblivious to the quality in such a scene that excites pity and sadness.

John Azzopardi did feel pity and sadness, but more than either of these he felt puzzled. Someone had killed the boy Hector Grech and in a terrible way. But it wasn't this ruthless quality that puzzled him, although it frightened him. There was something else that puzzled him, only he couldn't yet identify it.

He stood there thinking, gradually aware of the steady muttering of Amelia's voice. She was praying.

"She has need to pray," said the young policeman, returning with three coats and tossing them to the girls. "Here, take them."

"We all have need to pray," said John Azzopardi sombrely.

For some time now he had been conscious of men's voices outside the house, then he heard the heavy front door shut with a slam.

Two men came into the room. One, Sergeant Grima, was not known to him, but the other was his cousin Dr. Joseph De Bono, nicknamed The Inquisitor.

De Bono stood still and stared.

"John Azzopardi, you here?" He made it a question and indeed perhaps it deserved one.

"I came here to help," said Azzopardi, conscious for the first time that he was something of an outsider.

"But I'm glad to see you, glad to see you," and De Bono shook his cousin's hand warmly. Sergeant Grima also shook his hand, although silently, and less warmly –

"You used not to be *quite* so glad to see me," was John Azzopardi's reaction. But he tried not to be cynical. Perhaps his aunt was right; England had changed him more than he knew.

"But you shouldn't be here," went on De Bono. "And you're not dressed."

He looked a little shocked. He himself was neatly and precisely dressed in a dark suit with his necktie in a bow.

"He probably got his wife up to do that for him," thought John Azzopardi, remembering the legend in his family that Alice De Bono (who was another of his cousins, so inter-related are Maltese families) got up early in the morning to shine her husband's shoes. Involuntarily he looked down at the shoes and became aware that his cousin had seen his look and was amused. "So he knows the legend too," he thought.

"I only came to help," he said aloud.

"And now you must go away," said De Bono with perfect good humour.

John Azzopardi shuffled to the door suddenly very conscious he was wearing red bedroom slippers with a hole in the toe.

Amelia Grech suddenly spoke from the door.

"I like him."

The Inquisitor looked as if this was no recommendation. And indeed, in his opinion, far too many highly unsuitable people had liked John Azzopardi in the past already.

Sergeant Grima leaned forward and muttered something in De Bono's ear that John did not catch. Joe De Bono nodded.

"You can stay, John, if you like . . . You are a lawyer and my cousin. You've had experience in London, murder there, wasn't it? We might be glad of your help."

And the Sergeant's intervention could be interpreted, John Azzopardi said to himself cynically, as: "Let him stay. I've long wanted to make his acquaintance, and if we stay around long enough, who knows, he might talk?"

"Not murder," he said. "At least the courts decided otherwise: manslaughter."

In his opinion the judgement of manslaughter had been an easy way out for everyone. It had been a hideous and painful case in which a son had killed his father. John Azzopardi had been a witness, not to the murder, but to the sequence of events leading up to it: his testimony had helped to bring in the verdict of guilty of manslaughter but not of murder. There was a point in which provocation swung round from being a motive to being an excuse. But his experience had not enchanted him with life in London. You can be initiated too brutally into the knowledge that other people's lives are beastlike.

He had felt strongly that he was living in a non-Christian community; he had never felt this in Malta. But the episode had brought him a friend; he had met John Coffin, the London policeman.

John Coffin was almost Azzopardi's contemporary, perhaps a year or two older. The same events had shaped their lives; the war, the peace, the need to compete in a tough world. Almost without their noticing it, life in both their islands was changing beyond what anyone could have expected when they were born. John Coffin could remember a London in which trams had run, horse-drawn carts could be seen in the streets and men wore morning coats to work. John Azzopardi could remember a Valletta where great fleets rode at anchor in the Grand Harbour. Both worlds now belonged to the past. But Azzopardi's life had been shaped on principles entirely different from those governing John Coffin.

He had been educated at a school run by the Dominican Order, the headmaster of which was a charming and cultured man. He had seen his parents conform to certain rites. He had kept the great festivals of the church and had enjoyed the saints' day of his own parish with its fireworks and high jinks. Through all this he had been conscious of being a part of a community historically associated with the defence of Christendom against the infidels. He knew that he lived on an island circled with huge stone fortifications built by the Knights and dominated by churches and great cathedrals.

John Coffin, on the other hand, had been taught at a boys' day school in London, where the curriculum was as secular as the headmaster could make it, bearing in mind the provisions of the Education Act under which he worked. His mother was more given to card tricks than to prayers. He had educated himself, his university being, as Sam Weller put it, "the world". He had been unscrupulous, lying, tough and unkind. He had never been conscious of being a part of Christendom, but was very aware of being a man jostling around in a world full of other men, one little atom bouncing around in concert with a lot of other little atoms, all equally charged with positive and negative and some bound to destroy others. It was a salutary thought that since Rutherford no one's picture of the universe and its metaphysics could ever be quite the same. Coffin was perhaps more alert to this than John Azzopardi.

The result at the moment, considered John Azzopardi, was that John Coffin was the stronger, wiser, kinder character, and what conclusions did *that* lead you to? he wondered. But he had particular reasons at the moment for despising himself as a man.

"We heard about your murder case over here," said his cousin. "Or perhaps I should now call it manslaughter?"

"It was as near murder as makes no difference," admitted John Azzopardi.

"Except in the matter of the hanging . . . I don't believe in capital punishment."

"He wouldn't have hanged anyway, it wasn't capital murder . . . but perhaps the jury's decision was the right one, the boy had great provocation."

"I'm never sure what weight one should put on provocation," said Joe De Bono seriously.

The two lawyers stood for a moment in silence. Sergeant Grima coughed and brought them back to the room in which they stood. For a second both men were very conscious of the link their blood and profession gave them and Grima was the outsider; then Amelia Grech lumbered forward into the room, the picture righted itself and De Bono and Grima were once more the team.

If Grima noticed he had been momentarily in the cold he didn't show it but it was probable that he had not missed it; he was sensitive to things like that.

Amelia Grech spoke: "Get me a priest."

"There's enough people in this room already," said Sergeant Grima sharply.

"That's not the way to talk." Amelia came right up to him and stared at him. She was as tall as he was and more massive. "I want Father Vella."

"We're trying to conduct a murder investigation." The sergeant could be very anti-clerical when he was in the mood. At one o'clock in the morning, faced with murder and the need to assert himself against the Inquisitor, he was in the mood.

"You aren't conducting anything," said Amelia contemptuously.

"I'm starting now." He started to walk towards the other room. "Where's the body?"

"I'll tell you what has happened," began Amelia.

"No, don't tell me anything. I'll tell myself . . . No, don't touch," he grabbed Amelia's wrist and pushed her back.

"I have touched everything already," she screamed at him.

"Yes, she has," agreed John Azzopardi. Amelia's wrists looked very thick and muscular as she rubbed the one the sergeant had grabbed.

"It's a little late to be worrying about finger-prints now," said De Bono; he was not a scientific criminologist himself and set little store by finger-prints. He preferred a straightforward examination of the witness. Ask enough questions and ten to one, in the end, you got the whole story out. He didn't ask himself what happened in the one case where questions were not enough because he had met with one only once, and the difficulties *there* he was inclined to put down to the intransigence of his own cousin John Azzopardi.

"It's never too late," said Sergeant Grima. He had had this trouble with Joe De Bono before, and meant to stamp on it good and early. "Where is the constable?"

"Here, sir," said the young man, appearing from behind Amelia, whose figure obscured his.

"What were you thinking of to let her go round here

as she pleased. Don't you know better than that? Everything must be left."

"I couldn't stop her, sir." His face was pink. "Besides ... sir, she's his *mother*."

"Mother!" The sergeant turned round to Amelia. "Since when have you been Hector Grech's mother?"

"He is my own son."

"I always thought you found him in the bulrushes!"

"Now you are being insulting."

"Nevertheless, if he is your son, you are not married to his father."

"That will do, Grima," said De Bono. "Everyone knows these stories about Amelia Grech."

"Do they?" cried Amelia. "Do I know them myself?"

She is really magnificent, thought John Azzopardi. Not endearing, but magnificent.

"Where is my husband?" She looked round the room. "You can't talk like this in front of my husband."

"If you mean the man who is now on night duty at the R.A.F. Club at Sliema, he is not your husband either," said Grima.

"I am the mother of the dead child," shrieked Amelia: she drummed with her hands on her chest.

John Azzopardi wondered what it was that Sergeant Grima had against Amelia. Surely there was something more than mere clumsiness and assertiveness in his treatment of her. Somewhere in the past she had angered him. He looked at the tall erect figure of the sergeant and in his mind measured Amelia against him. The line between sexual antagonism and sexual attraction is known to be an unsteady one.

"Yes, over in there is his body," said the sergeant, pointing to the other room, "and that is where I am going."

He strode in.

"That's enough of that," said De Bono, mopping his forehead. "I can't bear his scenes, but he gets good results from them sometimes."

"He does?" John wondered if Joe De Bono really believed that the sergeant's outbursts of emotion had been entirely controlled and disinterested. "And what about the Grech girls?" he asked grimly. "What do they make of a scene like that?"

"Used to it," said De Bono shortly, preparing to follow the sergeant. Nevertheless, he told the young constable to take the girls to the neighbour upstairs.

Then he tried to explain the Grech family relationship to John Azzopardi. "All that stuff about Amelia – she *is* legitimately married to Grech, of course; he was her first husband's cousin. Same name. But there was a lot of gossip always about Amelia. She provokes it. And there may be something in it. The gossip was that the boy Hector was *not* her first husband's child. But is it true? How do I know? Perhaps Grima should not have taunted her with it." He added thoughtfully, "Oh, Alfred knows something I don't know about Amelia, I have no doubt."

"There seems to be a great deal to learn about Amelia Grech and her circumstances," thought John Azzopardi as he followed his cousin.

. . . . .

The inner room was crowded with furniture and poorly lit. There was light enough, however, to show the scene.

Dominating the room was a big brass bedstead. It stood with its head to the wall, jutting out into the room. There was a big cabin trunk at the foot of it which obviously served as a seat because it was covered with a blanket. On this blanket there was blood, a large trailing splash as if the bleeding head had been carried over it. Otherwise the room was strangely undisturbed, almost as if the killer had walked in and simply and neatly cut the head from the sleeping boy and walked cleanly out again. To John Azzopardi this increased the impression of a motiveless crime. "This is what *they* have done to me," Amelia Grech had said strangely, as if she was accusing the whole community.

He walked over to the bed. With a terrible simplicity Amelia had replaced the head on the trunk. Hector Grech lay there, arms and legs fully extended, and fully dressed.

"Did you find him like this?" asked De Bono.

Amelia nodded silently.

"Is this where he usually slept?"

"Sometimes."

A strange answer, thought John Azzopardi.

"But he was sleeping here tonight?"

"Yes," said Amelia. "He was there tonight. I looked before I went out."

"Did he usually sleep fully dressed?"

"Sometimes . . ." For the first time she looked flustered. "He was a big boy. I could not always control him."

"So? . . . and now, when he didn't sleep here on the bed, where *did* he sleep?"

"In the scullery," she said reluctantly. The scullery might account for the reluctance to undress, thought John Azzopardi.

"On the floor?"

"No. He had a bed there."

"So. He had a bed there. But tonight he slept here?"

"Yes."

Amelia was beginning to be resentful of this questioning. Her strength had supported her until now but now she staggered a little, and put out a hand to steady herself.

"It's cold in here," said De Bono broodingly, as if he had lighted upon an important point.

"I'm poor," burst out Amelia. "Poor. I can't afford to heat my rooms."

"It must be even colder in the scullery."

"Yes, perhaps that is why he came in here . . . I would have turned him out when I came in."

"Oh you would, would you?" said De Bono, eyeing her. "You that can't control him?" He moved away from the bed. "Grima, you can get on in here, if you like . . ." He turned to Amelia. "Mrs. Grech, *now* you can tell me what you know."

"What are they going to do in here?" demanded Amelia, lingering at the door.

De Bono shook his head and gave her a gentle push into the other room.

All through the conversation John Azzopardi had been made aware of undertones. Implications that he himself sensed but could not work out clearly. De Bono seemed to be getting at Amelia in some obscure way. He was building up a picture of the way the Grechs lived. But he was doing it in the manner of a man who thought he had already some idea of the way that was.

The boy slept in the scullery. Was that so funny? Perhaps lots of boys slept in sculleries. The fact was known about this boy because he was murdered. The thing about murder cases was the odd facts about the everyday life of ordinary people that came out.

All the same, De Bono's questions seemed directed at uncovering something connected with the Grech household. It could be interpreted as an oblique line of attack on Amelia Grech.

There was common ground between Amelia and De Bono here; he was attacking and she was expecting to be attacked. She was used to hostility. "This is what they have done to me," she said. Was she then so hated that her son must be murdered?

But De Bono's questions were already opening up another line of attack. Could she control her feebleminded son? Was he feared because he got out of control? And was he killed by someone who was frightened?

There were sexual undertones here. Hector, in spite of his mental slowness, had been a big, strong boy and might well have had an emotional development livelier than his mental age could cope with. John had a sudden picture of the terrified little maidservant he had found crying under the stairs. He wasn't even sure he knew her name. Was it Mary Colombo? But had she been frightened of Hector Grech? Physically frightened?

Joseph De Bono led the way back into the living-room and seated himself at the only table and sat Amelia Grech with her face towards the light.

"Now," he said in a commanding voice. "We will have your story." His cuff slipped back, revealing that in his haste he had forgotten his cuff-links. He glared at John Azzopardi and twitched the sleeve back into position again.

"What's he doing in that room?" persisted Amelia, nodding in the direction of the room where her son's body lay.

"Police business," said De Bono, settling himself with his pad of paper and pencil.

"Police business," repeated Amelia derisively. "Him?"

A small neat man came through the front door of Amelia's flat and nodded silently to De Bono. De Bono pointed towards the inner room; the man nodded again and went into the room.

"Now him too," said Amelia. "I ask you: what are they doing in there?"

"They have to discover exactly what happened to the boy."

"I can *tell* you what happened," cried Amelia. "But you don't let me. *They* too, all those neighbours of mine, ask *them* too."

"I shall, in due course."

"And see if they tell you," answered Amelia.

Sergeant Grima came through the door, murmured something to De Bono and sat down at his elbow.

"Well, let's get on with it," he said.

"You've left him in there by himself," said Amelia. "I know who he is; he's Dr. Muscat. What's he doing to my Hector?"

John Azzopardi suddenly felt very sorry for this bewildered, suspicious, ignorant woman. He leaned forward.

"There has to be an examination of Hector's body to check such things as when he died and what manner of weapon killed him . . ."

She was silent.

"Now you've cleared that up," said Joe De Bono ironically, "suppose we begin?"

Amelia took a deep breath. "I came back in," she said.

"No, begin a bit earlier. Begin with this evening." He looked at his watch. "Yesterday evening I suppose we must call it now."

In the yellow light from the gas-lamp, both he and Amelia seemed sickly and drawn. For all her size and strength, Amelia looked like a woman at the onset of a mortal disease.

"I was working late," she said. "I had a lot of washing and boiling to do."

"Who for?" asked De Bono quickly.

"No one, it was my own stuff. I'd got behind. I have a lot of washing for this big family. I always do it the night my husband goes off to his late night job."

"He doesn't go every night?"

"No . . . three times a week." She looked round the room. "He ought to be back by now, where is he?"

"Outside," said Grima. "He can come in when you have finished."

A glance passed between him and De Bono and Grima gave a little nod. As clearly as if he had shouted it, Grima had told De Bono that the husband was already being questioned.

"I wonder how long they've been married," Azzopardi thought, "and what sort of life it has been for them?" The room looked cheerless and poverty stricken but some attempt to liven it up had been made with a plant in a pot, and a bird-cage. Perhaps they had been happy.

"He'll be tired," said Amelia.

"Well, so are you." It was the first sign of sympathy either De Bono or Grima had made, and now it was offered by De Bono more as a statement of fact. "So this was how you spent the evening, in washing?"

"Yes."

"And Hector, what was he doing?"

"He was playing with his toys." She pointed to the heap of broken pieces of wood and metal which might have been toys in the long distant past before Hector got his hands on them. John Azzopardi thought he could recognise the wooden leg of a toy horse. If he thought anything at all, it was surprise that anyone had loved the boy enough to give him toys. They weren't very recent gifts anyway, he thought.

"And the girls?"

"They went to bed early," she said quickly. "They

always do. The eldest works in the kitchen at Ferrara's, the baker's, and she gets tired; she starts work very early in the morning. She took her little sisters to bed with her."

"So you were working alone?"

"Yes, on my own, in the scullery. Then Hector went to bed."

"In your bed?" put in De Bono smoothly.

"Yes, but I would have moved him when . . . later when I came to bed."

De Bono looked enigmatic. "And after your work you went out?"

"I was tired. And I thought I would like to see my friend Olive."

"Oh yes, I know your friend Olive Feltcher."

"So I went to see Olive and we sat together talking."

"And drinking a little perhaps?"

"Not much. Olive's mean."

De Bono had been writing carefully. "Before you left was the boy Hector all right?"

"I looked in the room before I went out. I could see him lying there. The girls were asleep too. It seemed all right to go out. And then, when I came I found . . . I found . . ." Unbelievably a tear trickled down her cheek. It was like seeing a tree crying.

There was a pause.

"Yes," said De Bono gently. "Now we must get the times clear. When did you go out and when did you get back?"

She screwed up her face in thought. "It was just after

half-past nine when I went out . . . I don't know when I got back."

"It was about ten past eleven when I was woken up," said John Azzopardi.

"It was seven minutes past eleven when I was telephoned by the man Fenech from upstairs," said Grima, speaking for the first time.

"He was lying there," said Amelia. "Well, I knew who'd done it. Someone from round here. They've killed him."

"That's a very terrible accusation to make," said De Bono softly.

Amelia did not answer. She looked sullen. She was not good at the come-back. She could be obstinate, insolent, she could even attempt the buffoon, but she couldn't answer back quickly. Now she just looked mulish.

"You must have some good reason for making it?" He went on, "What is it?"

"They don't like me. They talk about me." She hung her head and would not meet his eyes.

"Not enough," said De Bono, looking every inch the Inquisitor.

She believes emotionally in the truth of what she says, thought John Azzopardi, but does not believe in it as cold hard fact.

"Well, he didn't cut his own head off," said Amelia, at last.

"You've got to hand it to her," thought John Azzopardi, "when she does eventually find something to say, it has the ring of reality to it. He didn't cut his own head off."

The Inquisitor tried another line. "Is there anything special you can tell us?"

She looked blank and shook her head.

"Anything about yesterday? Anything that stands out? Or that might relate to your son's killing? Did he see anyone new? Quarrel with anyone?"

"No ... It was just a usual day."

"You must give me more help than you are doing. It was not a usual day. It was a day on which your son was killed."

A look of surprise crossed Amelia's face, as if she hadn't, somehow, quite thought of it in that light.

"Was there a quarrel?" he pressed her.

"No. No quarrel."

The Inquisitor abandoned this line, and after a whisper from Grima, tried something else.

"Who could get into this flat when you were out?"

"I never lock up," mumbled Amelia. "I have nothing to steal."

"That's not quite true. Your husband had this transistor radio," he pointed out. "And I suppose you had money sometimes."

"Not often. And it isn't his transistor, it's my eldest daughter's."

"Who knows that you never lock the doors?"

"Everyone knows I never lock my doors."

"In this house? Next door too? All your neighbours know too?"

She shrugged. "One person knew, anyway."

"And who could have known you were out last night?" he asked softly.

"They all could have known if they'd wanted to," she said sullenly. "But they were all asleep."

The Inquisitor sighed. "How often did you go out like this?"

"I don't know. Just when I felt like it. Sometimes. Not often."

"Had you been out at night this week before?"

She shook her head. "Don't think so."

"Last week?"

"Yes. Once."

"And was that also a night your husband was out too?"

"Yes," said Amelia reluctantly.

"And was that because when your husband was away you needed company or because you felt free of him and able to do as you pleased?" John Azzopardi asked himself.

"So in fact you were in the habit of going out to drink with Olive Feltcher when your husband was out?" said De Bono.

Amelia did not answer.

"And any number of people might have known that," he added thoughtfully.

The Inquisitor was establishing what opportunities there could have been for anyone to get in and kill Hector Grech. But he was also building up a picture, made up of hints and omissions, of the Grech family. The daughters who went up to bed early and who seemed of no importance to anyone. But the transistor radio belonged to the eldest girl and not to the husband. The husband had two jobs, one taking him out late on some nights; and when he was away his wife was in the habit of going off to see her friend Olive. Then there was the boy, Hector, playing with his broken toys and sleeping in the scullery. Finally there was the undoubted fact that when Amelia had asked about her husband and said he must be tired she had spoken with what sounded like affection. She had undoubtedly had strong feeling for Hector too. Granted that with a woman like Amelia Grech affection was still a tough rock-like emotion, yet there was no reason to believe the Grech family unfeeling. "Affection has as many forms as there are human beings," thought John Azzopardi, "and families are protean in their forms."

The Inquisitor leaned back as if he had run out of questions. He looked dejected. There was reason for his dejection. Murder was a rare crime in Malta. Now he had to handle an unusually unpleasant one. To get at the truth of Hector Grech's death he was going to have to turn over stones and uncover facts and unpleasantnesses that he would prefer to leave uncovered. Behind his tough exterior he liked a quiet seemly life. He was a man who valued deeply the decency and order of the society in which he lived; he never could have been happy in a corrupt and cynical society, he could not have lived in Germany under Hitler or in Imperial Rome. He liked to feel that he was in harmony with a well-ordered, kindly, honest universe.

Sergeant Grima interrupted with a question.

"Do you have an axe or a chopper in the house?"

Mercifully Amelia Grech seemed not to understand the implications of this question, and she answered without a tremble:

"Yes, I keep one for the wood."

"Where is it kept?"

"It is in the . . ." she hesitated. "It is in the scullery."

The scullery! There was something sinister about the way this room kept reappearing. Hector slept in the scullery, Amelia did her washing in it, and now it appeared the chopper was housed there too.

"We'd better take a look at the scullery." Grima stood up. "Mrs. Grech, you'd better go and see if your neighbour Mrs. Callus can take you in. You can't stay here." He held out his hand. "I'll go with you. Your daughters are there already."

Amelia did not move. "No." She looked obstinate. "I want to stay here."

"You can't do that," said De Bono impatiently. "The police have work to do here."

For some time past John Azzopardi had been conscious of the noise of voices outside the door which led to the hall. He had also fancied he heard an unobtrusive movement in the room where the doctor was examining Hector Grech. He fancied Amelia had heard them too. Every so often she had raised her head and half turned towards the door of the bedroom as if to hear what was going on in there.

The door from the hall suddenly opened and three

policemen came in, one of them the young man he had first met. Another of the policemen carried a camera and the third a small black bag. To John Azzopardi they were clearly the police technicians come to inspect the room. He wondered what his London friend John Coffin would make of the Valletta murder squad? They looked brisk and enthusiastic, anyway.

"You've taken long enough to get here," grumbled Grima. The Inquisitor looked displeased, as if he did not welcome this scientific invasion.

Amelia sat back in her chair as if it was going to take force to move her. It probably would, thought John Azzopardi. He wasn't sure if he blamed her. She was utterly bewildered, but determined to stick up for herself. And he was sure that in some inarticulate way she still felt the need to protect Hector.

Forgetting her for the moment, Grima led his men into the bedroom. John could hear him introducing the doctor and then the voices sank low and heavy. De Bono came round to speak to him. Amelia was staring through the open door.

"You'd better go off now, John," said his cousin. "I am going to send her away. Tomorrow we will ask some more questions. Today, I should say," he said with a sigh, looking at his watch.

"What do you make of it?"

The Inquisitor shrugged and raised his eyebrows all in one gesture. It was a characteristic expression of his. "Some sailor perhaps. They're all respectable around here."

Through the open door came the sound of a heavy thud and exclamations of dismay followed by movement.

De Bono looked sick. "The head's rolled off the bed," he said.

Amelia sprang to her feet and screamed: "He's not dead. His head's cut off but he's not dead yet."

At last her composure had broken. The three men helped her out of the room, and led her, weeping and struggling, up the stairs to the next floor. The woman who lived there opened the door.

"Bring her in, poor creature," she said. "Her daughters are here."

"Where's my husband?" asked Amelia, still crying.

"I don't know. Not here." She led the way into a small inner room and sat Amelia on a sofa. It was a neater, more prosperous-looking home than Amelia's. Amelia seemed aware of this because she shifted uneasily and looked self-conscious. Then she sighed and seemed to relax as if she was willing to stay. The other woman nodded her head and they departed.

"Did you hear what she said?" whispered the young policeman, as they went downstairs. "About the head, I mean?"

"Yes."

"She must be mad."

"She's a frightened, superstitious woman," said John Azzopardi. He raised his hand in farewell and made his way down the steps to where he lived. Although it was so early in the morning, not yet dawn, there was a feeling of stirring in the city. People rose early in Valletta. He went home and tumbled into bed.

Behind him he had left a house in which the axe which had decapitated Hector Grech had been found: under the sink in Amelia Grech's scullery.

Amelia, sleeping on the sofa in the flat above her own, snored. One of her daughters muttered in her sleep: "Hector, Hector."

And Amelia's husband, an emotional man, sat alternately weeping and raging.

III

John Azzopardi stared up at the great Caravaggio painting of the Beheading of St. John the Baptist which hangs in the Cathedral of St. John in Valletta. The cathedral is huge and dark but the picture springs from the wall with life and beauty. It is an enormous canvas, floodlit like a stage and highly dramatic. The Baptist is prone on the floor, his head extending in front of his executioner. Salome covers her eyes, the charger is ready to receive the severed head. The light comes from above, playing on their features, accentuating the agony and horror of the scene. Two men, their faces white and shiny, peer through a grille on the right.

The picture hangs in the Oratory. The Cathedral of St. John is a sixteenth-century building, its austere exterior concealing an inner darkness and richness. On the walls are baroque carvings, on the ceilings lavish paintings and on the floor are the ornate memorials to some of the important men of the Order of Hospitallers. You have to walk all through this big, sombre, decorated building to see the Caravaggio. Michelangelo Marresi, *il Caravaggio*, was one of the wildest and most violent of all great painters, as fated in his way as Van Gogh. Quarrelsome and drunken, yet genuinely devout, he was chased from Rome to Malta (where as well as his great painting of the Baptist he paint a fine portrait of the Grand Master Alof de Wignacourt). From Malta he fled once again to Italy, this time pursued by the agents of the Grand Master. He died in a drunken brawl in a tavern. All his knowledge of violence and brutality seems distilled within the painting of the Baptist.

John Azzopardi crossed himself and walked away. He never failed to be moved by this picture.

The building was full of tourists. A cruise ship had come into the Grand Harbour yesterday night (the night of Hector Grech's murder) and today Valletta was full of women with smart hats and good handbags and men with cameras. It was a British ship, the old *Argos Star*, home port Southampton; but the passengers were of mixed races, Americans and Germans predominant among them. Perhaps they only seemed to predominate, thought John Azzopardi, because they talked more. Anyway, the flower-sellers and the karrozzin drivers in the square outside were glad to see them and became lively and cheerful instead of sad and regretful of past days as usual. The karrozzin men whipped up their old horses and trotted up and down, waving their long whips and angling for custom.

John Azzopardi moved out of the dusk of the cathedral into the sun and light of noonday Valletta. On an impulse he stopped by a flower stall and bought a large bunch of anemones, blue and mauve and pink. He would send them to his aunt Baroness Castaldi, then he would go and pay his respects to his elder sister Fanny. Fanny had been a faithful loyal correspondent during his stay in England and would already be feeling a little hurt that he had not called. The thought of her six sons had put a brake on his eagerness to see Fanny, but it was still school term-time and all but two of them would be away from home. Unluckily the two smallest were, as he vividly remembered, by far the worst. All Maltese children are better behaved than English children, he told himself loyally, but Fanny's children might almost be American.

But, first, before Baroness Castaldi and Fanny, he had an appointment with another relative. He turned right at the corner of the square into Kingsway, strolled a few yards in the sun, and then walked into a café and sat down to drink black coffee, eat hot cheesecake and wait.

He had drunk two small cups of intensely strong coffee when the Inquisitor arrived. He was wearing yet another new suit and an even smarter shirt and carrying a black brief-case. He was also sweating.

He sat down at the table without a word, grunted and took off his sun-glasses.

"You are hot," said John Azzopardi sympathetically; he found himself liking his hot, bothered cousin.

"*Café*," said Joe De Bono to the waiter, and then to John Azzopardi, "Flowers, I see."

"Yes." John looked down at them and heard himself saying with surprise, "I am taking them to Chloe Zarb."

The Inquisitor's eyebrows shot up. He took his coffee

silently and drank it at once. Then he tapped the table impatiently.

"Well, make up your mind, either you're coming back here to settle down and build up a career for yourself, or you're going to take up with Chloe Zarb."

"This is only a bunch of flowers," said John Azzopardi. "At the moment all I am interested in is making a life for myself." There was a note of bitterness in his voice.

"For a man that means a wife, children," said De Bono. "You won't get that with Chloe Zarb."

Lily Castaldi had recommended him to celibacy, Joseph De Bono was offering him marriage and John Azzopardi knew that he was not in the position at the moment comfortably to follow either course. Perhaps Chloe *was* the answer.

"I know my own mind."

"I don't worry about you knowing your own mind," said De Bono, "providing you don't think you know other people's as well." He added, "You're not a confessor."

The word confessor gave him away; he was referring to the secret John Azzopardi had kept for three years now.

"So that still rankles?" he said.

"We never got the money back."

John was silent. Then: "I never thought the money was the most important."

"Twenty thousand pounds!" exclaimed De Bono, throwing his hands up. "You wouldn't speak so lightly if you were a married man with responsibilities and children."

Perhaps Joe's wife, his cousin Alice, in spite of her

family reputation of a devout slave to her husband was really a nagger, thought John Azzopardi, the way he went on about responsibilities.

It was a comment made with a sinking heart because he recognised that he was about to endure an onslaught from Joseph De Bono on the subject of the confession, as De Bono called it, which had been made to him three years ago and about which he had kept so obstinately quiet.

The onslaught came. "It was your duty to tell something."

"Oh, duty," said John thoughtfully. "It isn't always easy to know one's duty."

"It's always clear," said De Bono. "You can feel."

"You were thinking of the money, and I was thinking about people, that's the difference."

"There were people lined up behind the money. You forget them. The bank clerk who handed over the notes, the guard who was knocked out, even the policeman who failed to stop the car – they all come under suspicion, you pass over that."

"No." John Azzopardi was clear. "It was their job. Falling under suspicion was part of the risk they ran by taking those jobs. It did not fall on them out of the blue as it did on that unfortunate family. I was thinking of the family."

Joe De Bono was silenced; the family bond was one he respected. He recognised the power of the word. He sighed and drummed his fingers on the table.

"And remember, I don't admit the man said anything

to me before he died," said his cousin quietly. "I've always told you that much."

Joe De Bono smiled. "And you've always known exactly what I thought of that denial," he said. "However, perhaps I see a little better now why you said it."

The waiter brought them some more coffee and chased away a little boy begging for coins from an English tourist. The little boy didn't look hungry or poorly dressed. He looked a little sad and wistful perhaps as he departed penniless.

"They used not to do that," said Joe De Bono angrily.

"It's the Italian influence creeping in," said John Azzopardi lightly. He was sympathetic to the boy rather than angry like the waiter or shamed like his cousin.

"It's the Dockyard closing down," said De Bono. "There is unemployment, but these boys make it an excuse." He was outraged somehow that a fellow countryman of his, even so small a one, could be so lacking in self-respect.

"About Amelia Grech," said his cousin. "Where is she now?"

"She's in my office at this moment, repeating her statement; and then we are going to question her neighbours."

"An Inquisition, eh?"

"A correct questioning," said De Bono with a serious face, refusing to admit that he knew about his nickname. The Church had once kept an official Inquisitor in Malta and although he was a peaceful, gentle, administrator unlike his counterpart in Spain, perhaps De Bono did not relish the comparison. At any rate, no fires burned in his heart except a small discreet one for the better ordering of law and justice in his beloved island. He frowned. "I've managed to stop her going round making scenes and talking, but I can't stop the husband. He is going from house to house telling all his friends and neighbours." He sighed. "That's not the way to carry on. He's not the boy's father," he added abruptly.

"No." Azzopardi nodded.

"Carmel Grech only married Amelia two years ago. I started to tell you earlier. He was her first husband's cousin so she still remained Mrs. Grech."

"What happened to the first husband Grech?"

"He died about ten years ago in an accident. He was a man from Gozo and he went home visiting his family. He was drowned when the ferry sank on the way back. Her neighbours always said *he* wasn't Hector's father. By all accounts he and Amelia quarrelled all the time and there were plenty of other candidates. Not the way our women usually behave." He sighed. "Now you see why Amelia Grech is unpopular. She has earned her bad reputation."

"She's a beautiful woman in a way," said John Azzopardi.

The Inquisitor looked surprised. "You think so?" For his taste a woman had to be plump and rounded and feminine. "She looks more like a man than a woman."

"She could look like a goddess or a queen."

"What, a rough old washerwoman?" De Bono laughed, but he looked at John Azzopardi uneasily as if he really was dangerous. "You've been abroad too long."

"All I meant was I can see she could attract men."

"Well, she has." De Bono looked severe. His morality was strict and firm in sexual matters. He thoroughly understood and appreciated the way Amelia's neighbours felt about her and would have been shocked if they hadn't.

"And what about since her new marriage? Has she behaved?"

"Her priest says so," admitted De Bono cautiously. "I had a word with him. He keeps an eye on her, but she's been behaving all right . . . Comes to confession and mass regularly. No, she hasn't slipped there, she's very devout in fact, he says."

"I suppose he'd know?" asked John Azzopardi, thinking that Amelia might not be a bad actress.

"Oh yes, Father Vella has had a lot of experience . . . There is something odd, though." He looked round the room which was full of people smoking and drinking coffee, but no one was very close to them so he lowered his voice and said, "She hasn't had any more children."

"Is that so odd?"

"Well, think about it for yourself . . . She's not so old."

The picture of Amelia that was building up was certainly unlike that of the women of her class. They were respectable: she was not; they were fertile: Amelia, after an initial period when she certainly had been, apparently no longer was.

"What about the daughters?" he asked suddenly. "Where are they?"

"I've sent them back to the *casal* where Amelia came

from. The old grandmother still lives there. I didn't want them shouting their heads off too."

"An unlucky metaphor," said John Azzopardi.

De Bono winced. "Poor boy," he said, with genuine feeling. "Poor boy ... We shall have the doctor's report tomorrow perhaps."

He got up. John Azzopardi rose too.

"Well, will you come?" asked the Inquisitor. "I'm going to question the witnesses."

"As you have already questioned me?" said his cousin slyly.

The Inquisitor laughed, a little embarrassed. "Perhaps a little," he admitted. "I have the habit, you know."

And in companionable silence, they walked up Kingsway, past the ruins of the old Opera House to his home and office.

But Dr. Joseph De Bono, the Inquisitor, was wrong in thinking that all the Grech girls were safely away at their grandmother's house in the casal of Marsa Scala. Two of them were, one was not. They had certainly been driven out there early that morning in a police car, but the island has a good bus service and a bus had entered the village this morning and arrived at the station by the Phoenicia Hotel some forty minutes later. Rose Grech had travelled on it, and was in Valletta. Imprudent behaviour perhaps, but Rose Grech was a very frightened girl.

Rose and her mother were the two members of the

family who spoke English the best. Rose's English was fluent and almost unaccented; the nuns at her school had known her for a clever girl. In her way she was also a wise one.

At the moment, she was frightened for herself, she was frightened for her mother, she was frightened for the whole family. She feared actual physical violence.

She hurried through the streets crowded with shoppers. She was glad of the crowds because she did not want to be seen. She knew exactly where she had to go, but the clock near the bus station told her that she was in danger of being late. She started to hurry. She turned into Kingsway and then to the right again.

Her hurrying figure could, at this point, have been seen by Dr. De Bono and John Azzopardi who were just making their way to the Inquisitor's office. But they were deep in conversation and did not see her. In any case, it is doubtful if either of them would have recognised her; she looked quite different this morning in her coat and dress from the frightened girl of last night. She was still frightened, more so if possible after a conversation with her grandmother, but she knew she must not show it. "Don't show you are afraid," the old woman had advised her. "Try not to show you are afraid. Some people are worse if they see you are frightened."

Now she went plunging back into the district where she lived, where her brother had been killed and where she believed her family was hated.

She went quietly down the stepped street which led to her home. There was a policeman standing at the door, but he was dreaming in the sun and did not recognise her. The dogs sleeping on the grating and the cats prowling round the dustbins knew her, the baby sitting in its pram on the little balcony of the house next door knew her and smiled but no one else saw her pass.

She went round the corner and into the house where John Azzopardi lived, and called softly at the door, "Mary. Mary."

The little maid Mary appeared at the head of the stairs and peered down. She was the girl whom John Azzopardi had seen crying. She looked as though she had been crying since then without ceasing. Her eyes were puffed and swollen. She gave a startled cry when she saw Rose Grech, but she came down the stairs readily enough.

"Go away, Rose. Go away." She made a brushing movement with her hands as if she would push Rose away.

"I want to talk to you..."

"Go away, Rose. I am going home, it's time for me to go home." In the distance a church clock struck the hour. It was always a little slow, that clock.

"There is something you have to do."

"What is that?"

Rose gripped her arm. "Tell the truth," she said, "when you are asked. Tell the truth."

"Have – have told the truth."

"No." She gave the girl a little shake. "No. You haven't."

"I haven't said *anything*," cried Mary, beginning to weep.

"You like me?"

"I do, Rose."

"You trust me?"

"Oh yes, *you*."

"Then speak the truth." There was agony and desperation in the girl Rose's voice.

"I'm *afraid*," wailed Mary.

Rose was silent. She was up against a fear and awe greater than any she could induce. "So am I afraid," she thought sadly, "so am I afraid."

They were so preoccupied with each other that they did not notice the figure blocking out the light in the doorway and casting a shadow over them both.

Their walk up Kingsway to Dr. De Bono's office had been a kind of triumphal procession. The word had got round that he was back home in Malta, and John Azzopardi was surprised to find how many people had stopped to greet him.

First the tailor who had made his suits since he was a little boy taking tea with his mother and his aunt, the grand and beautiful Baroness Castaldi. Dark navy blue little suits they had been then, with neat, white shirts. He glanced down at himself. Still neat little, navy blue suits. And then an old friend of his father's, whom he had also known as a boy, jumped out of his car and involved his car, his chauffeur and two other cars in a traffic jam while he shook John's hand and welcomed him home. A man of his own age who had been at school with him crossed the road to introduce his wife. "Two children!" thought

John Azzopardi, "and he hadn't even met her when I went away." He began to feel like Rip Van Winkle. In the distance he saw Amelia Grech's husband pushing the covered hand-barrow in which he delivered her laundry. Work must go on.

"I didn't know I had so many friends."

De Bono grunted a little sceptically. He was rattling his keys preparatory to unlocking his door, he always kept his door locked, even when his secretary was working there.

"They're interested to see you, of course," he said. He had the door open and nodded to John Azzopardi to precede him. "I suppose they want to see what you've got to say for yourself."

"I don't think I've got anything much."

"That in itself will interest them. And then you've changed. Oh yes, you've changed."

"I have?"

"Oh yes. You went away a nice, affectionate young man, but a little soft and hollow inside. You've come back tougher, harder." He sounded cheerful, as if he thought the change for the better.

"But still affectionate," said John Azzopardi with amusement.

The Inquisitor's office was empty. His secretary had gone home to her lunch. She went early, at twelve, to eat soup and spaghetti round the family lunch-table with her mother, father, and five brothers and sisters. She was the daughter of an old friend and neighbour of De Bono's. She was willing, if stupid, and had left everything just as he liked it. A bottle of mineral water and a glass stood on a silver tray; his cigarettes were placed on a clean ashtray and today's newly arrived London papers had been placed alphabetically on his desk. *The Times of Malta* he had read with his breakfast.

"Ah, another London mass murder," said the Inquisitor with interest as he picked up the *Daily Express*. "What violence there must be underneath the surface there."

"On top sometimes," said John Azzopardi. He too was studying the newspapers. The three deaths of the three women had taken place in the part of South London he knew. "I think I know the man who'll be investigating this, a man called Coffin." For a moment he was back in London and could hear that deep, rather sardonic voice saying, "Lovely murders we have here, why don't you go back to that island in the sun of yours where you never do?" "We have a little violence here ourselves," he said to his cousin.

"Oh, but nothing like what it is there." De Bono was settling himself comfortably at his desk. "You're thinking of this affair at the moment, but there is no comparison, none at all. When we get to the bottom of it we will find it very minor, very trivial and probably an accident."

"I don't think any case that has Amelia Grech in it could be called trivial."

"What I mean," said the Inquisitor then, thoughtfully, "is that it will turn out to be the result of a chance act of brutality, isolated, trivial in *that* sense, and not reflecting any real disorder in the community." He looked up at John and smiled.

"He really believes what he says," thought John Azzopardi. "I hope you're right," he said aloud. "But perhaps no murder is really a chance act of brutality." "And I believe what *I* say," he thought with slight surprise. "Murder does always spring from something more than chance. Or perhaps what I really mean is that there is no chance." He stirred uneasily in his chair, not quite liking the thoughts that were coming to him.

The smell of food floated down from the De Bono kitchen on the floor above and the Inquisitor looked wistful.

"We have just time for a quick bowl of soup before the first witness comes in with Sergeant Grima . . . if we hurry," he said, swallowing. "It's fish soup: I smell it is fish soup."

"I'd love a bowl of Alice's fish soup," said John Azzopardi truthfully; he would also be amused to see his cousin in his family milieu.

"I was up at six, busy all the morning at my private practice," said De Bono, getting up and hurrying cheerfully to the door. "Six children and a wife take some keeping, John."

"All at school?"

"All at school except the little ones . . . But Alice manages beautifully; I am a lucky man to have such a good wife." As he spoke he was nipping up the stairs followed by John Azzopardi. The smell of *calamai* and *lampuki* mingling beautifully with onion and tomato grew stronger. They had reached the kitchen.

Alice De Bono was surprised and pleased to see John; he noticed, though, that she was not equally surprised and pleased to see her husband. Indeed, Dr. De Bono, now actually within his wife's presence, had a distinctly hangdog air.

"I thought you'd be glad to see John," he said, as if anxious to ingratiate himself. He picked up a piece of bread and nibbled it. "We've come for a bowl of good *Zuppa di Pesce*."

"Yes, it's ready." Alice gave the soup a stir. She wasn't loosening up at all, though, John noticed. "I'll pour it out."

"How are the children?" asked John as he drank some soup. The Inquisitor was right. Alice's fish soup was superb. He thought she had added a dash of saffron to it, in the Venetian fashion. His cousin was guzzling the soup up greedily but still keeping a wary eye on his wife.

"Well," said Alice, but she frowned.

"A touch of trouble there," thought John Azzopardi curiously. He couldn't believe that any of those quiet phlegmatic little boys were behaving badly. If it had been Fanny's children now . . .

The telephone rang in the room next door and the Inquisitor went to answer it, having first looked hopefully at his wife.

"Speaking," they heard him say. "Oh good, so they've finished down there. No, I don't suppose you did get much in the way of finger-prints, but you'll have to check . . . No, take my advice, don't let Amelia or her husband go back, they can go on staying where they are . . . Yes, with Mrs. Callus – if she'll have them."

There was a rumble from the telephone.

"No, I don't suppose the neighbours *do* want them there, but where else are they to go, ask yourself that . . . We can't put the pair of them in prison just to oblige the neighbourhood . . ."

There was another rumble.

"No, the girls are safely out in the country with their grandmother. Yes, come right down, I am waiting for you."

The Inquisitor came back into the kitchen and went on with his soup.

"Sergeant Grima," he said, between gulps. "Having trouble with Amelia Grech. They can't go back to their own home yet and the neighbours don't want them."

"Anyway, Amelia says one of them killed the boy," said John.

"So she does," said the Inquisitor with a frown. "Most unlikely."

"The murderer must have come from somewhere close by," said Alice, covering up her soup.

"Oh, that's what you think?"

"That's what I think," said Alice.

And once again John was aware of the tug between husband and wife. They were not quarrelling. Alice was too gentle and well-mannered, but she was asserting herself and De Bono was placating her. It was interesting.

"You know we haven't yet any idea in the world why

anyone should kill that boy," said the Inquisitor thoughtfully.

"I think anyone who knew him might have killed him," said John Azzopardi, considering that uncontrolled figure he had seen walking in the street. "In a panic, in an accident or out of fear."

"I am perfectly certain that whoever killed him knew him well," said Alice.

"In other words," said the Inquisitor, "you two both accept Amelia's accusation: one of the neighbours killed him."

"Yes," said John Azzopardi, after a pause. "Yes, I believe I do."

Alice De Bono went back to stirring her soup; she said nothing.

The Inquisitor, John Azzopardi and Sergeant Grima sat round the table and smoked. The preliminary investigation into the murder of Hector Grech was under way. In front of each man was a pad of paper, a glass of water and an ashtray. So far John Azzopardi's pad of paper was bare, but his ashtray was full. There was nothing on his cousin Joe's pad either except the large numeral "I" but Sergeant Grima appeared to be drawing one of the steatopygous models to be found in the Valletta museum. He looked up and blushed when he saw John Azzopardi's eyes on him.

"That was what I heard," repeated the man who was being questioned. "That was what I heard." He shifted uneasily in his chair.

"Nothing?" said the Inquisitor. He now managed to make the word sound incredulous. He's really very good at this, thought his cousin. "You're not deaf or anything. All that noise going on and you heard nothing."

"Nothing," said the man with conviction. "I buried my head under the pillow and heard nothing."

Azzopardi thought of the cry of rage and rejection with which his London friend Coffin would have greeted this remark.

"Very well," said the Inquisitor smoothly, but with a faint sigh. "Go back to before where you started to hear nothing and tell me all about it again."

A confused sound of loud voices broke in from the room outside. In this little ante-room were sitting some of the people whom Dr. De Bono and Sergeant Grima were questioning. There had already been some argument about the order in which they should be questioned. De Bono had been precise but firm: he would decide whom he wished to see according to the logical reconstruction of events. Sergeant Grima had merely shouted "Wait," in a loud voice.

Now the sergeant leapt to his feet and disappeared from the room abruptly, banging the door behind him. The room beyond at once went quiet.

The witness already in the chair crossed himself.

"He thinks Grima has the evil eye," explained the Inquisitor in a whisper.

"So he has," said the man. "Anyone can see."

They sat in silence for a few minutes. John Azzopardi thought that the evil eye must be a useful attribute for a policeman, and perhaps Sergeant Grima did not discourage the idea.

The sergeant came back into the room. "Settled that," he said.

John observed that his eyes were a bright, beautiful hazel, unusual in a stock predominantly brown-eyed. There was a cold glint in them.

"It was the Grech man . . . says he must get on with his work . . ." One of Grech's many jobs was to deliver the laundry of Amelia's customers. "Says he has to deliver out in the country."

The sergeant sat down. "He borrows a van . . . He only gets the van once or twice a week."

"Work must go on," mused the Inquisitor. "And it would be hard on the people who were expecting their laundry."

"Yes." The sergeant put his hands on his knees comfortably "So I said 'Yes'. I told him he could go out. He'll be back by the time we want him."

A surprising man, reflected John Azzopardi. He likes Grech. His feelings towards Amelia are ambiguous, but he likes Grech. For Sergeant Grima it would always be a man's world.

Waiting in the room outside sat the elderly woman Callus, who had taken in Amelia and her daughters last night. She was a widow. Close beside her smoking and reading a newspaper sat the man to whom John Azzopardi had spoken outside the house last night and who had cried out, with blood on his face, that it was difficult to be kind to Amelia. His wife nursed their infant child. Another man and a younger woman sat together by the window whispering, and the little maidservant Mary stood against the wall with her sister. They did not talk, but occasionally they looked at each other.

Seven people to be questioned and no doubt there would be others, but these were Amelia's closest neighbours. John Azzopardi had wondered if it was usual for people waiting to be questioned in a case to be gathered together like this, or whether it was something Grima and his cousin had thought up for this particular group, some form of pressure perhaps, or whether, as he strongly suspected, Joe De Bono was a law unto himself.

Suddenly the man reading the newspaper screwed it up into a ball and threw it into the middle of the room. His companions looked at him silently.

"We can't say it," he cried. "It's no good. They won't believe us. We can't say." His wife put her hand on his arm and he sank back into the chair. She was calmer than he was.

"Questions, questions," he muttered. "I'm not a clever man, I don't like questions." He fumbled for words. "I don't know what to say. Give us the facts, that's what they'll say. But what are the facts?"

There was a pause, then he started up again: "Questions. I'm not good at questions."

"Don't speak at all then," advised his wife. She looked capable of carrying this out herself, but he couldn't.

"I'm frightened," he said, almost weeping. "You're all frightened too. But I'm the only one who admits it."

But by their very silence they all admitted it too.

Within the next room the inquisition had begun again.

"Now," said the Inquisitor, picking up where he had left off. "Let us start again at where you heard nothing."

"It was like this," began the man. His hands were trembling.

Out in the country, in the casal of Marsa Scala, two Grech sisters sat together quietly with their grandmother. She had lit one small lamp. She had no electric light. She did however have a radio set which was playing now as it played all day.

One of the girls was sleepy, but the other, who was next in age to Rose, was fretting. Suddenly she spoke:

"Where is Rose?"

Her grandmother sat weighing up the question in silence for a few seconds.

"She's gone into Valletta," she said in her deep solemn voice. She went on with her sewing.

The girl looked about her. It was late, it was dark.

"Yes, but Grandma," she persisted, "where is she *now*?"

The standard of intelligence was much higher in the younger generation of Grechs than in the old.

The First Inquisition

IV

The Inquisitor had certainly observed that the man's hands were trembling and if he had not then Sergeant Grima's silent, prolonged stare at them would have told him. But he said nothing. His voice grew neither gentler, as John Coffin's might have done in the circumstances, nor tougher.

"And your name again, please?"

"Michael Green." He was still trembling.

"That's an English name."

"My father was English, he is dead now, but my mother is still alive. I've never been to England. We were going once, in 1939." He was silent again.

"That's right," said Sergeant Grima.

"Of course it's right. I don't know why you ask me. You know it."

"He knows. I didn't," said the Inquisitor.

"Then you should have known it. I've delivered newspapers to your home every day for the last twenty years."

"And that is your job?"

"No, that's not my job," he said impatiently. He added

proudly, "I am a messenger. In the Ministry of Education. The newspapers I do in the morning."

"And you live in the house in which the Grech family live? On the floor above the one on which this terrible murder took place?"

"Yes." Michael had relaxed now. "I have a room at the back."

"And yet you heard nothing?" said the Inquisitor gently with that half smile he had and which this witness seemed to find most intimidating.

"Nothing." He mumbled the word. "I was asleep. I go to bed at eight o'clock."

Eight o'clock was not uncommonly early by the standards of his class in Valletta. He went to bed early and got up early. He spent the day walking about on poorly shod feet, carrying the messages and parcels which were handed out to him. The job of messenger was a humble one and not well paid, but it carried a small pension and a certain status. He was a Government employee. He had a uniform. But when evening came and he was alone, the uniform was not much consolation for loneliness. You could hang it up and look at it but you couldn't talk to it. And Michael loved to talk. He had talked to Amelia Grech and even the boy, Hector.

"Hector was my friend," he said suddenly. "He was a nice boy, you know. I understood him."

"You did?" the Inquisitor asked.

"Yes." He repeated with satisfaction. "I understood him ... I mean I never went too far."

The simple menace implied in this statement seemed to escape him.

"Then who did?"

"Eh?" He shook his head. "I don't understand."

"Who did go too far?"

There was no answer.

"Someone did," explained Dr. De Bono patiently. "Or was it Hector who went too far?"

"Now you're confusing him," said Sergeant Grima.

"About yesterday," said the Inquisitor. "You were in the house, you knew the Grechs, you were a friend of Hector's. Did you hear anything that surprised you?"

"Oh no," said Michael, grateful perhaps not to have been surprised.

"Nothing that sounded like a murder or a quarrel? Or a fight?"

Their eyes met. Michael said nothing, then slowly shook his head. "But of course, I forget," went on Dr. De Bono. "You had your pillow."

"You keep asking me the same question," complained Michael.

"It's the only one I want an answer to. Oh, you can go now. Perhaps I'll see you later."

Michael got to his feet. Sergeant Grima whispered something.

"Wait," called De Bono. "Were you in the Grech flat yesterday? No? When were you last there?"

"I never go in," said Michael simply. "Amelia didn't like it."

"Let the sergeant take your finger-prints then, please, before you go."

"Oh no, I couldn't do that." Michael put his hands behind his back and closed his eyes. "It's not right. No, you can't touch my hands."

De Bono and Sergeant Grima looked at each other. Then Sergeant Grima smiled.

"Can you write, Michael?"

"Oh yes." He was pleased. "The nuns said I wrote a beautiful, clear hand."

"In English too?"

"Yes, and read it. I have a little English diary." Proudly he produced a small red book. It was four years out of date.

"I thought I saw one." The sergeant stretched out a great brown hand. "Here, I'll have it." He slid it neatly into his pocket. "That'll give me your prints."

Michael Green puckered up his face with unhappiness. "My book," he said. "You can't have it. I want it."

John Azzopardi was touched. "Give it him back."

"He'll get it back. I won't harm it or him." The sergeant was unperturbed. "You've got soft in England." He gave Michael's hand a little pat. "You'll have it back tomorrow."

Michael accepted this, as he did so much else in his life, with dignity and an almost complete lack of understanding.

"England would have been nice," he said to John sociably, as he prepared to go. "Still, the war wasn't bad either."

"I'm glad you thought so," said Dr. De Bono whose office had been blown away with a bomb, nearly taking him with it. Sergeant Grima had served in the British army.

"It was interesting," said Michael. "Things happening. Things to talk about."

John Azzopardi smiled at him as he went out, suddenly seeing things through his eyes. It was a small world, smaller than Malta, no bigger than the limited observation of Michael. There were many things he did not see, many he did not understand. A childlike, unpolluted world. Yes, in that world you *could* put your head under the pillow and hear nothing.

"Is he telling the truth?" he asked.

De Bono shrugged. "How can I tell that *yet*? He is a man who normally speaks the truth, I think, but on this occasion perhaps he has reason not to."

The sergeant slapped his pocket. "This little book may make interesting reading."

"I don't know how many inhibitions of the lawyers' code you broke whipping that off him," observed John.

"I'm not a lawyer."

"I can't believe he kept a record of anything."

"I bet he wrote something in it," said the sergeant shrewdly. "You'll see." He flipped the pages over. It was true enough, here and there a few scrawled words appeared.

"Wait a minute," said De Bono suddenly, "call him back, there's something I want to ask."

"He has done this often," thought John Azzopardi.

Grima went to the door and shouted, but Michael was brought back with some difficulty. Having once been in the inquisitorial room he had hurried to get away from it and he was already out of the door and away down the street. He was brought back looking sulky. John Azzopardi saw that he was a man of more varying and uncertain moods than he had supposed. He was not always a good child, he could be a bad child.

"When did you last see Hector Grech?"

"I don't know," he mumbled sulkily.

"Yesterday?"

"I don't remember."

"Did you quarrel?"

"I didn't see him."

"So you *do* remember something."

"I mean I didn't see him yesterday evening," said Michael, even more sulkily.

"When *did* you see him?"

"I don't remember."

"If it wasn't the evening then it must have been in the morning, you're at work all day. Was it the morning?"

"I did see him in the morning."

"For how long?"

"Eh?"

"Did you talk? Were you with him for many minutes?" said the Inquisitor patiently.

"I don't know how you knew I saw him." He sounded cross.

"You've just told me so."

Michael was silent. Then:

"He walked a bit of the way to work with me. He often did that." He smiled, sweet again. "We talked."

The Inquisitor leaned forward. "Michael, did you see him when he was killed?"

A strange way to put the question, John thought.

"No," said Michael. Somehow he seemed to get the edge on this question.

"Did you see him once he was dead?"

"No."

"Do you want to?"

There was a silence.

"Yes," said Michael. "Yes, please. I have some flowers for him."

It was perhaps not the answer which the Inquisitor expected.

Rose Grech moved her head slowly from side to side. It ached badly, more than she ever remembered it aching before. She was as strong and healthy as a little pony and hardly knew pain.

"I've been kidnapped."

But no, somehow the word kidnapped didn't quite fit the case and blearily she knew it. What had happened to her was more complicated.

She wasn't sure exactly where she was. The blow which had knocked her out had muddled her.

She was constricted, in the dark. Rose put her hands out in front of her and touched. What she touched felt cold and slightly damp; she thought it was wood. Her hand fell back and touched something soft.

"Perhaps I am in my tomb and this is my shroud," she thought. Rose was not normally a girl given to morbid thoughts and even now she rejected this one as soon as it was formed. "No, I haven't been buried. I can hear noises."

She could hear a voice in the distance. "All right. *Buona notte. Saqa.* Carry on."

"Help," she shouted. "Help me, Rose Grech." But only a tiny little bleat came out. "I am Rose Grech," she muttered to herself, anxious to cling on to the only thing she was sure about.

She had confused memories of the blow that had fallen on her head, of a face leaning over her. She could not remember the details of the face but it had been a familiar one, the sense of that remained with her. She remembered her fear.

"Mother," she had tried to call. "Mother, help me."

What she forgot was why she had been attacked. If she died now she would not know the reason for her own murder.

The next person to be questioned was the man who had been reading the newspaper and who had cried out that he was frightened. No one in the Inquisitor's office had heard what he said, but perhaps they were not entirely unaware of it. Sergeant Grima gave him a hard look as he came in. John Azzopardi, more sensitive but naturally less observant, only thought that the man looked reluctant to come into the room. Sergeant Grima had detected the actual signs of fear, of clenched hands and of rigid neck muscles and interpreted them correctly. He had questioned this man once already and knew that he was deeply disturbed and unhappy. He scribbled a message on a piece of paper and passed it across to Dr. De Bono. The man saw him do it and his mouth opened with apprehension.

"He has more on his mind than just this murder," read Joe De Bono. He nodded and folded the paper. "But they all have," was his thought, "so have I, so have you, it's the way life is." He knew very well that Grima was preoccupied with something, and as for his cousin John Azzopardi his life was loaded with problems, except that John seemed to carry them lightly. He gave him a faint smile.

His witness interpreted the smile as meant for him and relaxed a little.

"I ought to get back to work," he murmured hopefully.

"What do you work at?" asked De Bono, clinically, like a physician asking for the symptoms.

The man tightened up again at the tone. "I'm a hairdresser, sir."

"They won't miss you for a little while." He looked at the man's hands, wondering if those hands, skilful with a knife and scissors, could have decapitated Hector Grech. "In the Bazaar down by the fish market, is that where you work?"

The man nodded.

"Have you lived long in the same house as the Grechs?"

"Two years. Since I married. My wife lived there before that."

De Bono nodded. "Good neighbours, eh?"

"You can't be a good neighbour to Amelia, she won't let you."

"He's got a grievance there," thought John Azzopardi, suddenly alerted. "This makes the second time he's said the same sort of thing."

"She doesn't like you?"

"No, it wasn't that quite." He paused to think it out. "It's that she takes her own way. Yes, that's it," he said, as if satisfied that he had got the phrase right. "She takes her own way."

"So I suppose that means you don't like *her*?"

"No one can make me say that," cried the man. "And I won't say it. I don't say whether I like Amelia Grech or not. Remember that, I don't say."

"And Hector Grech? Did you like *him*?"

"I don't know anything about Hector Grech." The questions had driven him to sullenness. John Azzopardi was puzzled as he looked at him. He was a young, respectable looking man, he had a gentle face, he was not stupid but he was behaving like a primitive, ignorant man. He was sounding the same notes as Michael Green, but Michael Green was dull-witted, this man was not: he was intelligent and tense. "Nothing to know about him. Animal."

De Bono nodded without comment. "So, where were you on the evening of the crime?"

"I was at home."

"Doing what?"

"We had supper. I played with the baby." He shifted his eyes from face to face.

"It was a quiet evening?"

"As usual."

"Quiet down below?" De Bono leaned forward. "Also as usual downstairs in the Grech flat?"

John Azzopardi studied the piece of paper on which he had scribbled the names of the witnesses due to appear. This man was called Peter Fenech; he was a hairdresser. He was twenty-six. He was married with one child.

"I didn't notice. I was playing with the baby."

"How old is your baby?"

"Six months."

"That didn't take all night then," said De Bono decidedly. "You had time to take in things."

"Such as the murder taking place down below," put in Sergeant Grima. "You were sitting just up above playing with your baby. Didn't you hear something?"

"No."

"It must have been a very quiet murder," said the sergeant bitterly. He was beginning to get angry with this type of witness.

"Yes, it was," said Peter.

"I suppose your wife was with you all the evening?"

"Yes."

"Did either of you go out at all?"

"We never left our home."

"Did anyone come to see you? Is there anyone who can bear witness that you two were there, as you say?"

"There's my wife."

"Anyone else?"

Eventually Peter said: "Mrs. Callus, our neighbour. She came in to see the baby; my wife had been worried about it because it cried."

Sergeant Grima made a note. "I shall ask her about that," he said.

Mrs. Callus was Amelia Grech's hostess of the night before and John had a clear memory of her worried, honest face.

"She will tell you it was so."

Grima didn't answer. Instead: "And now I want to take your finger-prints."

Peter held his hands out obediently.

"So that doesn't worry him," thought John Azzopardi. He and the Inquisitor looked on silently while the sergeant performed his task. It was soon done.

Peter stood up. "Can I go now?" He looked at the sergeant and the sergeant looked at the Inquisitor. Dr. De Bono fidgeted with his papers.

"You say your wife lived in this house where you now live before your marriage?"

"Yes." The word came out reluctantly.

"In the same flat?"

"No."

"Where then?"

"Downstairs."

"Downstairs? Where downstairs? There are only two flats there: the Axisas' and the Grechs'. Was it the Axisas'?"

"No."

"Where downstairs then? The Grech flat?"

"She lived with the Grechs," said Peter slowly.

"Did she? You'll have to tell us more than that. Why did she live with the Grechs? Just as a lodger?"

"No."

"What then?"

"She's Amelia Grech's sister."

"So – your wife is Amelia Grech's sister and this is the first time you tell us."

When Peter Fenech had gone Sergeant Grima said: "Did you notice the bruise on his nose and left cheek?"

John Azzopardi said: "Amelia Grech gave him that bruise. She struck his face the night of the murder."

Grima raised his eyebrows.

"Does your bruise worry you, Peter?" asked his wife timidly. "I notice you touching it."

"Yes. It worries me." He touched his face. "Of course it worries me." He added, "It's not the pain but the way it happened. You understand that, don't you? It's the way it happened."

She muttered something he could not hear.

"I'm not a Cyclops then, am I?" he said. "I can't be all eyes."

"Cyclops?" She'd never heard of Cyclops. "You sometimes don't see things."

"I have seen enough." He gave a visible shudder.

His wife put out her hand to his uncertainly. The developing relationship between them had included affection and desire but understanding had not so far made much progress. She knew what to do when he was happy but was bewildered when he was not. Lately they had both been unhappy.

"I'll cook some *lassagne* when we get home," she said.

"Home?" His voice rose. "Haven't you grasped it: we haven't got a home."

It was her name that Sergeant Grima called politely next time and he helped her into the room with the baby.

But inside her the conversation continued: But we have a home, of course we have a home. Nothing can touch people like us. We are innocent, Peter and I. No one could blame us for what we did – are doing, corrected the accurate little censor inside her.

At this nip from her conscience she gave a small groan and Sergeant Grima looked up.

"You feel ill?"

"No." She shook her head.

"There's no need to be frightened," said the sergeant, a little alarmed. He preferred questioning men to women, especially women with babies. "Now let me help you sit down. Is the baby all right?"

"Oh yes, he's asleep."

"Big boy for six months," said the Inquisitor; he knew about babies.

"Yes," she agreed warily.

"So the boy Hector Grech was your nephew?"

"Yes," she said, even more warily.

"It must have been a very great shock to you when he was killed."

"Yes." But she didn't speak with conviction.

"So you really expected something like this to happen?"

She opened her mouth in silent surprise.

"I can read between the lines, you know," said the Inquisitor. "Did you hear anything that night that could have been the murder taking place?"

"Oh, no." "Nothing must touch us," she was thinking. "I must protect Peter and my baby."

"You heard absolutely nothing?" asked the Inquisitor, shaking his head from side to side as if in sympathy. 'When did you first know Hector was dead?"

"I . . ." she swallowed, "I, we heard people talking on the stairs. My husband went down."

"And that was the first moment?"

"Yes," she said again, with that strange, disquieting note in her voice.

"So there you were in the middle of the night, aroused by voices, you learn of your nephew's death, but you don't seem sure it was a great shock. Are you sure this was the first you knew?"

She stared at him with great deep-set brown eyes: she was dumb.

But her other voice was not. The words formed themselves into a great clear shout within her: if we say nothing we are safe. *Provided we do not speak no one can ever know.*

"Oh yes," said Alice De Bono speaking on the telephone in her own comfortable sitting-room upstairs. "He's here, Chloe dear, down below with Joe and Sergeant Grima . . . Well, between us, Joe is hoping John will come into partnership with him and wants him to get experience . . . Yes, the Grech case."

At the other end of the line Chloe Zarb said something which her cousin (for Alice and Chloe were cousins too) answered.

"No, it must have been a sailor, a stranger anyway. That's what I think, Chloe." Alice reached out and pulled forward a pad of paper on which Joe had been scribbling. "Finger-print?" he had written. Finger-prints, she thought. *No, finger-print.* Still smoothly talking to Chloe, she took a pencil and scribbled out what her husband had written. Somehow she didn't like the thought of that finger-print.

"No, Chloe," she said. "I won't call John to the telephone. Although for you I'm sure he'd come." They both laughed, but in Chloe's case a little sadly. "I will tell him you telephoned."

Poor girl, poor girl, she thought, as she started to replace the receiver, no child, no loving husband. Then she remembered that there were problems even for happily married wives with loving husbands, and scowled.

"Oh, Chloe," she called. "Chloe." But Chloe was already gone and the line was dead.

She started to laugh, her earlier mood of gloom and anger dissipated by this conversation with her cousin. It was all very well to think of Chloe as a poor girl but when you did this you forgot that Chloe could be tough and resilient. No one who dressed with Chloe's expensive dishevelled elegance could fail to have a strong sense of her own identity. You might call it a sense of her own style. And perhaps a drunken husband and a tragic past was a necessary part of it.

"I'm a cynic," Alice thought. "How surprised Joe would be." She was a little surprised herself.

The atmosphere in Joe De Bono's office had changed. John Azzopardi could tell that his companions were getting more and more uneasy.

"They don't like what is coming out," he told himself. "And yet *nothing* is coming out."

Then he corrected himself. Every witness had protested that he or she knew nothing. But this in itself was gradually assuming significance. It was unnatural to be so ignorant.

"We'll see the older woman, Mrs. Callus," said De Bono to Grima, and then to John, "You'll find her interesting. She's a good sort of woman. Speaks lovely English and Italian. Her mother was an Italian opera singer, they used to come over and do a season of operas in the old days as you know." He sighed. The old Opera House still stood, bombed and in ruins, at the end of Kingsway as it had stood now for twenty years and those old enough missed the gaiety and brightness of the winter season as they had once known it. John Azzopardi nodded: he remembered being dressed up and taken by his mother, also dressed for the occasion in pearls and satin, to sit in Aunt Lily Louise's family box. Aunt Lily Louise had worn the Castaldi tiara of diamonds and emeralds and had glittered more than the Governor's wife. "Anyway, Mrs. Callus's mother married a Maltese wine merchant and settled down here. She died during the war, cursing Mussolini."

"What's Mrs. Callus doing living in that house then?"

"Oh well, it's a perfectly respectable comfortable house; you mustn't go by the way Amelia Grech lives. Mrs. Callus has lived there for years. I believe she owns it."

Mrs. Callus looked tired and uneasy as she sat down. But she was polite. "I'd be glad to get back as soon as I can, if you please, Dr. De Bono. I still have Amelia Grech and her husband staying with me and I didn't let her have the key to the front door."

"It was good of you to take her in, Mrs. Callus."

"I like to do my duty. Besides, Father Vella told me I must."

Joe De Bono scowled; he was sometimes guilty of anticlericalism and would rather have thought that it was at his wish Mrs. Callus had sheltered the Grech family than at Father Vella's.

"I used to hear your mother sing when I was a boy," he said. "I suppose I was about eight or nine, but I remember her. A lovely woman. Beautiful top notes."

Mrs. Callus smiled. "She wasn't really very good. She sang in that over-produced florid Italian style – it wouldn't do today."

"But that's what I like. I love Verdi and Puccini." He felt pained at her implied criticism. Opera to him meant Italian opera; there was no other.

"I expect if you heard her company today you would think it pretty poor," said Mrs. Callus; her taste in music was more austere – she liked Bach and Mozart.

"Oh no," said Joe De Bono, shocked to hear stones being thrown at one of the memories of his life. Music, culture, civilisation, they had up to now been epitomised by those yearly winter visits of the Italian opera company. Now he was told it was second rate, if not third.

"I like *bel canto*," said John Azzopardi. No one took any notice of him.

Sergeant Grima coughed.

"Ah well, back to business," said the Inquisitor. "You visited the Fenechs last night?"

"Yes. The baby cried. But there was nothing the matter. Peter worries too much."

"You are the baby expert, Mrs. Callus?"

"I'm Mrs. Fenech's friend. I'm sorry for her; she has two babies: her son and her husband."

"You've known Mrs. Fenech a long time?"

"Oh, a long, long time." She sighed. "Since she was a girl. She's only one now."

"And at this time it was just a normal evening, nothing to alarm you?"

She shook her head.

"Now what can you tell us, Mrs. Callus, about this dreadful business?"

"Nothing," she said without hesitation.

"But there was a murder committed, just on the floor beneath you. You must have heard something? Sensed something?"

"Nothing. I was playing music on records. Loud. I could have heard nothing. As to what I sensed, I am not a sensitive person. Who can sense murder anyway? What a question."

"Yes, Joe *was* rather carried away with that one," thought John Azzopardi with amusement.

"In any case," went on Mrs. Callus, "the Grechs were a noisy family. If I did hear anything I would think nothing of it."

"You don't like to have them living in the same house as you?" asked Sergeant Grima suddenly.

The question had slipped under her guard; for a moment she remained silent. Then: "No." Her hands started to tremble.

She hated admitting that, observed John Azzopardi, it has destroyed all her self-confidence (which he now saw his cousin had very cleverly bolstered up; he took back his criticism of Joe's questions to her: they had been skilful).

De Bono suppressed his exasperation at Grima's clumsy intervention.

"I have heard that the boy Hector liked you and would visit you sometimes?"

"Yes." Mrs. Callus smiled, one lip twitched nervously. "Poor boy. He was quite musical. Strange, isn't it? I was almost fond of him in a way."

"I'm glad someone was," said De Bono.

"What do you mean?" Her voice was sharp.

"He was murdered, wasn't he? Someone killed him."

"Oh, but it must have been a stranger, a sailor," said Mrs. Callus; she was beginning to breathe irregularly.

"No. I think he knew the person who killed him," said De Bono sadly. "Did you know that there were tears on his cheeks. He had been crying just before he was killed."

Mrs. Callus moaned and toppled over in her chair.

"She has a bad heart, I think," said John Azzopardi leaping forward. He lifted her up. "Get some brandy, Grima."

"Yes, I know she has," said Joe De Bono, not moving. "But this time I think she has just fainted. I didn't expect it to do this to her."

"It upset her, she was fond of the boy."

"But not that fond, surely? Not even his own mother fainted." He seemed stuck to his seat, hypnotised by Mrs. Callus's reaction.

"The brandy, Grima," said John Azzopardi, holding out his hand. He was thinking that Amelia Grech had done something much worse; she had projected her fury and despair and given it a voice, a gait, made it live.

Sergeant Grima quietly took Mrs. Callus's fingerprints. "Pretty hands she has," he said. "Poor silly woman."

The next person in the room was the girl, Mary Colombo. John Azzopardi smiled at her, but she stared back through swollen, red-rimmed eyes, without relaxing her air of anxiety. "Crying again," he thought. "I don't think I've ever seen that girl without tears." She blinked at him and he thought that in addition to tears she probably couldn't see very well; she had short sight. Then she recognised him and gave a timid nod. But she did not speak. At no time in the interview that followed did she speak freely; words had to be forced out of her. After ten minutes Joseph De Bono began to show irritation.

"Come along, my girl, you can tell me more than this," he said, tapping his desk with his pencil, like an impatient schoolmaster. She responded to this automatically as perhaps he had known she would.

"I am trying but I have nothing to tell," she said in her longest burst of words so far.

"You live with your sister, you both went to bed early and you heard nothing," said Dr De Bono, recapitulating briefly from his notes. "Still you knew *something* had happened, you must have done, you got up and came down the stairs."

"That was afterwards," said the girl, and then stopped short.

"After *what*?"

"After we knew he was dead."

"Go on," said the Inquisitor in an expressionless voice.

"We heard the voice of the policeman – and Mrs. Callus banged on our door. It was safe to come then."

The Inquisitor let what she had said hang in suspense for a moment. Then he leaned forward and spoke:

"You realise what you are saying to me, you silly girl, is that you and your sister *did* know something was very wrong in the Grech flat and that you deliberately did nothing about it?"

Mary stretched out her hands towards him as if she

would like to shut his mouth, close it against the words that were coming out at her like weapons. A long red weal started to appear down the side of her jaw as if it had been whips and not words he had used.

"You must tell me," he said in a stern voice.

"We did hear something . . . but we were frightened." She hung her head and would not look up.

John Azzopardi had a vivid picture of the two girls in their crowded dark room, huddled together in fear.

"What sort of something?" asked the Inquisitor, but in a more gentle voice.

"Oh – voices – shouting," she said, still not looking at him. "Noises."

"Bad enough to frighten you?"

"We were frightened."

"That I believe," thought John Azzopardi; "she has been frightened and is frightened. She looks as though she has been frightened for weeks."

"But when was this noise?"

"I'm not sure. I don't know."

"After you went to bed or before?"

For some moments she did not answer, but when Dr. De Bono pressed her she said: "Before, I think."

"And so you went to bed *after* hearing the noise?"

"Yes." She was flustered.

"I suppose it seemed safer," said the Inquisitor sarcastically.

"It probably *was* safer," said Sergeant Grima, speaking for the first time.

Mary looked at him warily; the red mark on her face

was still clearly visible and looked sore. She put her hands on her lap and held them together to stop them trembling. They were red and stained with the dirt worked into the skin and round the nails.

"Only seventeen and her hands look like that," thought John Azzopardi.

"Did you see any of the Grech family yesterday?"

"Only in the morning. I saw no one in the evening."

"Did anyone see you? Is there anyone who can say that you and your sister were in your room?"

"Mrs. Fenech. We take our meals with her. Peter is our cousin. We had supper there then went to our own room."

"Peter Fenech did not mention you being there."

"We ate early. He came in later."

"Mrs. Fenech did not mention it either."

"It's true, all the same." The girl showed her first flash of anger. "True, true, true."

"So you came in from work, had your supper and went to your own room?"

"Yes," said Mary Colombo.

"I'll have your finger-prints, please," said Sergeant Grima.

"And this noise which you did not investigate, did it sound like anyone you knew? Did you recognise the voices?" put in the Inquisitor.

"No. I recognised nothing," said Mary Colombo. She shook her head. "I don't see very well."

"It's your hearing that's in question." The Inquisitor frowned at her. "Was there something you could have *seen*?" he asked with a hint of a pounce, like a cat for a mouse.

"No. I saw nothing."

"That's not very convincing, my girl."

"Your finger-prints, please," said Sergeant Grima patiently.

"You looked out of the window, did you?" said the Inquisitor suddenly inspired. "You looked out of your window and saw something or someone?"

"Yes," whispered Mary. "I saw someone climbing out of the ground-floor window." She said it with relief.

"She's glad he asked her that," decided John Azzopardi. "It is the only question she has been glad to answer, the only one."

"You see quite a lot," said the Inquisitor dryly. He leaned back; he too had detected her relief and wondered if she was lying.

In the next hour they questioned the other Colombo girl, the Axisa couple, recalled the Fenechs and questioned them about the noise of shouting which Mary Colombo had heard. But they got nothing out of it. Even Helen Colombo shrugged off the question about the noises. She was made of tougher stuff than her sister, was older and wiser and warier. John Azzopardi saw how sensible his cousin had been to question the younger girl first. He was coming to respect Joe's professional skill, even while retaining a wry question mark about the values which ordered his life. Perhaps in private Joe was not so happy and successful as he seemed. He began to think Joe a more complicated creature than he had once believed. His left eye was twitching now.

Joe De Bono saw him looking and lit a cigarette irritably; he placed a hand on his eye and held it there momentarily. It did tremble and he knew why it trembled. The tremble was his warning signal that something was wrong; that somewhere along the line his system was overloaded. He was a successful lawyer, a brilliant public speaker, with his eye on politics; he might yet be an independent Malta's first representative at the U.N., he was a careful and responsible husband and father; but it was too many lives to live up to. Of the symbiotic lives existing within him he was wondering which was the real person. The buds of all his selves were withering.

"Well, John?" he asked sharply.

"I wondered about the finger-print. Why were you both so interested in this finger-print?"

"We have one," said Joe De Bono but without giving more information. "Was that *all* you thought?"

"You got nothing decisive. You lost the impetus halfway, I think."

"Amelia Grech is not respectable. She does not live well. There was much quarrelling in her house. I know that, all these people must know it too. But," and he banged on the table, "not one of them is willing to admit anything. Not even willing to admit they heard anything.

"Except the girl Mary Colombo. And I don't know what to make of her except that I don't think she's telling the truth." He added thoughtfully, "I'm almost sure she's a liar."

"Yes, she's a liar," said Sergeant Grima.

"I think so too," admitted John Azzopardi, "although what sort of liar I'm not sure."

"There's only one sort," said Grima.

"Apart from her, silence," said the Inquisitor. "They witness each other's alibis. All except Michael Green – *he* only had his pillow. Otherwise it might be a conspiracy."

The word fell like a stone into the silence.

"There's something they all know," said Joe De Bono. "That woman Callus knows it, Amelia Grech knows it. You get glimpses of it underneath all the time."

"What is it?" John asked.

"I can make a guess," said his cousin grimly. "It relates to the character, habits and relationships of Hector Grech."

Alice De Bono was coming down the stairs as they walked towards the front door. Her husband slowed down and stood waiting for her.

"Going out, Joe?"

"Just walking a few yards with John."

"It's cold, Joe," and she smiled at him. "Here, take this scarf." She removed the soft silk from her throat and placed it round his neck.

"Oh, thank you, Alice, thank you." He looked at her with gratitude and affection also; John Azzopardi decided, with relief that Alice had thawed. The scarf impeded his breathing and the evening was muggy but he wound it round and round enthusiastically.

"Good-bye, Alice," John held his hand.

"Chloe Zarb telephoned for you. She wants to see you."

The Inquisitor grunted, but in his new mood of amnesty allowed it to take on a friendlier note.

"I'm looking forward to seeing Chloe."

"One always is," said Alice. "It's been her undoing."

The front door opened very slowly.

"I came back," said Michael Green, to Dr. De Bono. He was carrying a very small bundle wrapped in a silk handkerchief. "You told me I could see Hector?"

"Yes. If you want to. Later."

"Not today? I have brought his bird." He unwrapped the bundle and displayed a limp canary. "It's to bury with him."

"Did you *kill* it?" asked De Bono in horror.

"No," Alice De Bono spoke. "He did not kill it. It died naturally."

"Yes," Michael was matter-of-fact. "I went back and found it lying there dead. It was in its cage on the stairs. I suppose they just forgot to feed it." He seemed unconcerned, as if *they* might easily do as much, and more, to him any day.

V

The sun shone on the stone buildings and narrow streets of the old Birgù of Vittoriosa where John Azzopardi was walking with Chloe Zarb. The old town across the Grand Harbour retained its attraction for John, who had lived here as a little boy. When the Knights Hospitallers first came to Malta they found only two towns on the island; the old capital up in its hill, Mdina, and the Castello on the Grand Harbour with its little Birgù or borough clustering behind it. The military order ignored Mdina and concentrated on fortifying the Castello and its Birgù. The Castello became the great fortress of St. Angelo which rears its stone head up into the sky, dominating the Grand Harbour now as it has done for centuries. The Turks when they came in 1565 wasted their forces against the strength of St. Angelo all through the long summer of the Great Siege. When it was over the little town of Birgù was given the name of Vittoriosa for its fortitude. Since then it had withstood yet another great or even greater siege and survived. But not without destruction, thought John Azzopardi, remembering the bombs.

"I withstood a Great Siege here myself for that matter," he said thoughtfully.

"The war, you mean?"

"No, not the war, although I was here then and so were you, Chloe." He smiled at her. "No, it was just after the war, the summer I was seventeen. We still lived here then; the old house hadn't been sold, or what was left of it, it was badly bombed, you know. Perhaps it was living in its shell that affected me, or perhaps it was the war itself, or perhaps it was a real genuine feeling I had. I've never been sure." He was silent for a moment.

"I think all your feelings are true, genuine ones," said Chloe Zarb in a gentle voice. She was dressed in a plain, dark-blue, linen suit.

"Yes, but I have too many of them."

"I am perhaps prejudiced," agreed Chloe with what would have been a giggle in a less attractive woman. "I like emotions, more and bigger and better emotions."

"I know you do, Chloe," said John Azzopardi. "That's your trouble."

They turned up a shady side street, away from the motor-cars and the bicycles, and walked towards the graceful church of St. Lawrence with steps leading down to the water, and the elegant church of the Hospitallers which stands next door to it. There is a little terrace in front where they paused for a while.

"I like this place," said John. "It makes me feel tranquil and civilised."

"You are civilised," said Chloe. "That's *your* trouble."

"You don't say tranquil, I notice."

"No." Chloe shook her head. "You're not tranquil. Not yet."

"Not you either, Chloe?" said John Azzopardi with an inquiring look.

"Not me either," agreed Chloe. "But we were talking about you. And the long summer of your discontent."

"Was it discontent? Yes, perhaps it was. It didn't seem like it at the time, but you may be right. I was seventeen and I wanted to become a monk. I thought I had a vocation. My mother said 'No'."

"So you were on the grid-iron like St. Lawrence?" said Chloe, with a backward flick of her head towards the church.

"I debated it all that summer. I stayed behind here. All the rest of them went off to Gozo. It was quiet here. Not much traffic. We were still short of everything here then. And there I was all alone, reading poetry, listening to music, hungry most of the time and trying to renounce the world. It must have been quite a comedy."

"A lot of things seem a good joke afterwards," said Chloe Zarb, with bitterness.

"The commotion I caused. There was my mother sending letters and my uncle Castaldi sending priests. My mother's motive was clear enough; I was her only son and she didn't want me hidden away in a Trappist Monastery, which was what I romantically fancied . . . About my uncle, I don't know. I imagine he was acting on instructions from my Aunt Lily Louise."

"He usually was, wasn't he, poor old man?"

"He was a very happy old man. Aunt Lily Louise made him terribly happy."

"Oh, you only say that because you're a man."

"You know the thing with you is that you're exactly like Aunt Lily Louise. I suddenly see it." Two beautiful and bossy women, he thought.

"She'd faint if she heard you say that."

"She knows it, I expect. She knows everything by now, Aunt Lily Louise."

"Not quite everything," said Chloe mildly. She was looking and smelling delicious.

"Where do you get your clothes, Chloe? I never see another woman here who looks like you do."

"I go to London and Florence. London for my winter clothes and Florence for my summer ones, the Italians are better for the summer; I would prefer to go to Paris for both, but that I can't afford to do." Chloe spoke in a serious voice as if on a subject to which she had given earnest thought, as indeed she had.

"London and Florence," said John Azzopardi, shocked. "Chloe, the expense!" He was a frugal man and wore his own clothes till they were in holes. Even Aunt Lily Louise never went outside Valletta for her clothes; he thought Alice De Bono made her own.

"Oh, I do understand why you nearly became a monk," cried Chloe. "You don't understand the world at all. You ought to be in a cloister! But you aren't nearly nice enough: they would never have had you in."

"I don't think it's niceness that counts towards holiness. Look at Father James Nicholas, an old horror but really devout. Anyway I decided my mother was right. By the end of that summer I knew that she was right and I was wrong." He laughed, looking back on the years behind him. "Oh, how wrong I was!"

He turned to Chloe with a smile.

"And I suppose that was also the summer when I fell in love with you, Chloe."

The wind blew up the steps from the water as they walked towards it.

"Oh, so it was," said Chloe Zarb as if it was something far away and forgotten that she could hardly remember.

As it probably was, thought John Azzopardi, and for him too that summer was ancient history and long ago. He felt the tightening of the muscles of the stomach that heralded his memories of what had happened in the years between. "I never knew before," he said to himself, "that unhappiness is a real pain precisely located. Chloe knows, I suppose. Poor Chloe, you never had a chance for all your pretty clothes, and air of being brave: you're just not clever enough. Even the woman I am thinking of is helpless and she is clever."

He was immediately precipitated in thought back to his recent meeting with the Baroness Castaldi.

They had met by the statue of Queen Victoria on her empty fountain which stands in the handsome square outside the great library. Then they walked up and down the colonnade which runs round two sides of the square, talking and sheltering from the sudden showers of rain. Baroness Castaldi was carrying a rose in a pot and looked like a mixture between Cinderella's Fairy Godmother, and with the angry glint in her eye, the Wicked Fairy.

"So you're meeting Chloe Zarb," she said at once. "Already."

"Only for lunch," he said, not bothering to ask how she knew.

"And afterwards Chloe will say let's go and look at the Museum or walk with me to my hairdresser's."

"*With* her husband," continued John, ignoring her last comment.

"He won't stay the course," said Lily Louise Castaldi, who had also taken an interest in racing in her youth. "He never does. Either he won't turn up or he'll go away early with a headache which by that time he'll have from all the wine he's drunk."

"You're just building up my interest in Chloe."

"Oh, I did think you'd be too occupied and busy with this terrible murder case you're helping Joe De Bono with."

"So that was your idea too. That's why Joe De Bono had his arms wide open in welcome."

"Not at all. If Joe goes into politics seriously, as he may well do, as I *pray* he may do, then of course he wants someone to take over his law work for him. It has always been a family practice."

"You do me too much honour, Aunt," said John Azzopardi, suddenly angry. He wanted to shatter her composure and iron certainty. "There's nothing Chloe can do to me, nothing."

"Ah, I wondered why you left London. There was someone there?"

"Yes."

"And why did you leave her?"

"She had a husband already."

Baroness Castaldi looked sad. "So you couldn't marry her. Ah, well, for us there can be no divorce."

"I wanted to; I would have been glad to, I thought none of the ideas I'd been brought up with mattered, but I found I couldn't."

"I can understand that."

"Can you? I couldn't. But we lived together for two years. My virtue didn't go as far as abstinence." His voice shook.

Lily Louise Castaldi looked troubled. "But you came home. You gave her up."

"She gave me up. She wanted to marry me."

He came back to the present to find Chloe standing waiting for him to walk on; she looked pretty and patient.

"We're two for a pair, me and Chloe," he thought and took her arm. But as he walked on he had to admit that Aunt Lily Louise had been right about one thing: he was spending the afternoon with Chloe.

"If we go this way," she said pointing, "we can see the Inquisitor's palace, which I very much want to do."

"Is that why you brought me out here?"

"Yes, I suppose it was really. It's being restored and redecorated, did you know?"

One of the nicest things about Chloe, as he now remembered, was her genuine feeling for buildings and pictures. She took affections for houses, groups of old buildings and she went back to see them and kept an eye on them just as she would have done a circle of ageing friends.

"The old house on the corner is having its roof repaired," she would report. Or, sadly, "Another shutter gone from the house in Castile Square, and I'm afraid the rain is getting in. It'll soon be too late."

John had the feeling that in taking him to see the Inquisitor's Palace she was paying him a high compliment as though she was introducing him to an old and cherished friend.

"I always think he must have been a very moderate, gentle Inquisitor, our Inquisitor in Malta," said Chloe as they approached the neat unobtrusive sixteenth-century façade. "He lived in such a civilised, domestic way. It's really just a charming town house and as for his country palace it's one of the loveliest small houses in the world, I think."

The Inquisitor's Palace, deserted and partly derelict, was under reconstruction. The workmen had left the gate open and they walked inside and stood looking about them. The house was built round a small square inner court. Grass was growing there now and it was deserted. A workman had left a barrow upside down beside a pile of bricks. It reminded John of the man Grech pushing his heavy barrow up the slope.

"Wonder how the Grechs are," he said aloud to Chloe.

"Those are said to be prisons over there," said Chloe, who knew her way about. "But I don't feel he was a really serious prison keeper, do you? I mean, when you think of the prisons of the Doges of Venice." She shivered. "Now they *are* prisons."

John Azzopardi peered through a partially blocked door into a dark pit. He could see another door set in the wall next to it. A faint, sweet, rotten smell rose up to his nose. He frowned. "Unlike you, Chloe, I don't know that I do think them such desirable residences." He was almost sure that behind the closed door he could hear faint sounds of movement. He put his ear against it. There was a faint dry rustle.

"Do you hear anything, Chloe? Can you hear a noise inside there?"

Chloe listened, then shrugged. "Perhaps a rat? Or noise from the workmen?"

"Perhaps." He turned away. They left the courtyard and walked up the handsome flight of stone steps to the piano-nobile where the Inquisitor had lived with his staff. But once or twice he looked back down to the deserted prison.

In spite of what Chloe said, there *was* something sinister about them.

It was, however, utterly impossible, surely, that there should be anyone in them now? Then why did he have this strange worry stirring in his mind?

Dr. Joseph De Bono listened on the telephone to Sergeant Grima. At the same time he could hear his typist fumbling away at her typewriter in the room beyond, and Alice banging her pots and pans in the kitchen above.

Today he felt tranquil and restored. Alice had forgiven him and she said it was all due to Chloe Zarb. He didn't quite understand how Chloe Zarb came into it and hoped that Alice had been discreet (but she would have been) in what she had told Chloe. But now that he was on good terms with Alice again he had to admit he was very happy.

"Primitive but natural," he told himself, humming a little tune and hardly listening to Sergeant Grima labouring away in explanation on the telephone. But come to think of it Grima sounded happy too. Or if happy was too relaxed a word to use of Grima, you could say he sounded satisfied and eager.

"Now it's this way, Dr De Bono," said that keen voice. "I've got the report on the finger-print and a preview of the medical report and I have news."

"Yes?" said De Bono, euphoria rapidly departing.

"You recall the finger-print? The special one?"

De Bono recalled the finger-print. There were, of course, any number of finger-prints in the rooms belonging to Amelia and her family but there had been one strange extra print. Sergeant Grima was rightly proud that his men had found it at all.

The finger-print, that of a forefinger, was on a tablet of ordinary household washing-soap, the sort you might use to scrub a floor or clean out a sink. The tablet of soap had come from a wooden box on a shelf in the famous scullery. Amelia Grech said it was always kept there. But it had been found on a table by the door of the flat as if left there in flight. That was one explanation anyway.

The nature of soap being so evanescent, it had followed that the print must have been left on the tablet at a time when it was still damp enough to retain a good impression and yet before it could be worn away in use. This restricted it, so the Sergeant had argued, to the few hours after Amelia had done her washing that night. He believed that the print could only have been made at this time. From this it followed that it had probably been left by the murderer. To himself the sergeant put it even more strongly. "Find the owner of the print and you have the killer," he had said to himself.

"Yes, I remember the print," said De Bono, "the one on the soap? You've found who made it?"

He had never himself placed much store by the solitary print, having seen even more promising pieces of evidence lead nowhere at all in his time. Privately he had thought it very unlikely that the sergeant would ever get a positive identification at all.

"Yes," said Grima, "we have. And it changes everything ... The print belongs to the girl, Mary Colombo."

"I see your trouble," said De Bono. "It is difficult to believe she had physical strength necessary to kill the boy. Or the motive," he added.

"I'm not sure about that," said Grima. "She could have had a motive all right. She was frightened of him. Plenty of people say so. People who could know. If she was frightened of him, she might have attacked him in panic."

"If he attacked her first," said De Bono, not liking the direction his thoughts were taking.

"Yes, there would have to be that first."

"And then, she's in his own home attacking him," went on De Bono. "So *he* didn't seek out *her* company; she went after him. The print is there in the Grech flat and so is the body, not in some alley or dark corner."

"I agree it doesn't make a straight picture."

"It doesn't make any sort of picture," De Bono went on. "If she killed him in a panic, then she wouldn't have done it in his own home. If she did kill him in his own home then it wasn't in a panic."

"I don't think she did kill him," admitted Sergeant Grima. "I know I said once whoever left this print was the killer, but now I think this girl left the print and still wasn't the killer."

"She was there on the spot. I'm beginning to wonder how many other people were there on the spot too?" ("This child may have been the focus for the murder," he thought, "she and her fears may have triggered off the explosion that she was not the killer . . . Was there more than one person involved?" he asked himself.)

"You have something else, Grima?"

Sergeant Grima could hear him breathing heavily, hopefully, at the end of the line and hardly liked to be so brutal as to tell him the truth. "The old man believes too much in human nature," was how he put it to himself. "This is going to turn him up."

In certain moods he always called Dr. De Bono "the Old Man". They were moods of anger and scepticism. There was a deep division between them, that of politics. Grima sometimes felt that he and De Bono, although both Maltese, were on different sides. He had often wondered if De Bono knew all the reservations that existed between them. The Old Man was clever though; he probably did. Now Grima thought: "My mind is full of things that I don't want to tell him about."

Grima was thirty-five, nearly eight years younger than Joe De Bono. He came from Zabbar, his father had died young and his mother was poor. But she had only the one child and what money there was went to his upbringing and education. Alfred Grima was clever and industrious; he was also ambitious. The police force offered itself as a ladder for his ambitions. He was also an honest man and this occasionally he had found a disadvantage. John Coffin of London could have told him that policemen everywhere find honesty sometimes a disadvantage, but he could have added the worldly wisdom that, in the end, dishonesty is even less of an advantage.

Grima felt separated from Joseph De Bono by education and background. "He is one sort of Maltese and I am another. He is loyal and patriotic but he has taken so much from the English, he is more like them than he is like me," was his not altogether unconscious expression of this separation. "He is rich, and I am poor; we have different ambitions, different interests."

Amelia Grech and her family (and hence the murder in it) were different things seen through Joe De Bono's eyes and then through Alfred Grima's. To Joseph De Bono the woman Amelia Grech, although she was his countrywoman, was almost alien, a person whom he had to make a conscious effort to comprehend, he could not do it instinctively, he had to learn her language. "And he doesn't always speak it very well," thought Grima wearily, "he speaks Maltese with an English accent." Literally, of course, he knew this to be untrue, Dr. De Bono was completely bilingual, but emotionally it had some reality. Because of this emotional fog he did not see Amelia Grech and her neighbours clearly and could even use the word conspiracy of what he saw. But Grima knew that the lies and evasions, which were certainly taking place, might be the result not of a plot to deceive but of fear. He admitted, however, that all the signs were that it was a common fear, one which all shared. What this fear was he did not yet know. It might quite simply be a fear of him, Grima. He knew how his reputation for toughness ran in Valletta. Amelia Grech and her neighbours were simple, stupid people and Joe De Bono was making them too complicated. He was also, Grima felt, making them too obscure. When they finally got the truth about the murder it would be simple. It might also be brutal. Brutal.

"You're not going to like this," he told De Bono. The disparity between them loomed larger than ever. "Amelia Grech and me on one side of the divide and him on the other," Grima thought. The Grech case seemed to cut across his prejudices at many different levels like a trench. But he still didn't like Amelia Grech.

"Go on," said Joe De Bono. The rough treatment his typewriter was getting in the next room had finally convinced him that even although his secretary, Edith, was the child of his best friend and client she would have to be replaced by someone with a gentler hand on the keyboard. He was a man who respected machines and liked them to be treated with sympathy. He winced at the thump and rattle from next door. "Well? I'm listening."

"Perhaps I shouldn't tell you on the telephone," mumbled Grima. "It's the medical report on the boy Hector Grech."

"It's helpful, is it?"

"Let's say it gives us a different picture from what we expected. The first thing is the actual cause of death itself. You noticed there wasn't all that much blood about, I suppose?"

"I did."

"Killed by a blow on the head which injured the brain and made him first unconscious. This was the actual death blow."

"I see."

"They think he may have lived for some time *after* the blow."

"But unconscious?"

"Yes, almost certainly didn't die at once. May have been capable of movement. You see where this is leading us?"

"I'm trying to."

"Head decapitated in one clean blow. No extensive haemorrhage from cut veins, no firm coagulation, and complete absence of coagulated blood infiltering the tissues. The edges of the wound are not swollen," he was reading rapidly from his notes, "no signs of blood spouting and apparently even more important, no sign of leucocytric infiltration into the clot. The blood on the head and trunk was washed away easily."

He did not need to explain further.

"He was dead when his head was cut off," said the Inquisitor bleakly. "He had been lying there unconscious for some time, he died, and then someone cut his head off. Why? And why does it make it worse?"

"It does though. Also makes it bloody complicated." Grima rarely swore. De Bono did not like to hear it even now and coughed awkwardly. "We have to think of the time scheme now. There was some time between the first blow and death and then decapitation."

"Amelia Grech was out for some hours."

"He must have been attacked some time after she left and then *later* the killer cut his head off. Why?"

"It suggests more than one person involved," said the Inquisitor straight away, "which is what I always thought. They're probably all in it."

"It suggests more deliberation and less panic," admitted Grima.

"We have the finger-print of the girl Mary Colombo, proving she was on the spot."

"We have something else as well." Sergeant Grima consulted the précis he had made.

"How unpleasant all this scientific evidence is," thought De Bono.

"This is the real stuff of detection," thought Grima as he rustled through his notes.

The gulf between them yawned wider.

"First of all, there are signs of blood in the *scullery*. Not too much, but some."

"Where?"

"Yes, that's the point." Always bang on the nail, the Old Man, acknowledged Grima. "On the sink, on the water-tap, on the rack where the towel hung and on the door."

"In other words the murderer washed himself, or herself, clean."

"I think that is part of it; but there are other stains in the bedroom which are elongated, like a bloody exclamation mark." The sergeant was never poetic and De Bono realised he meant what he said literally without appreciating the vivid image he was evoking. But both men understood the implication of the shape of the bloodstains.

"So he was carried into the bedroom still bleeding from his head wound, and probably before death?"

"Must have been."

"A nasty picture," said the Inquisitor sadly. "Attacked in the kitchen, carried into the bedroom. He dies. And then his head is cut off . . . We must try and keep it quiet."

"I can keep some of it out of the papers. Not all."

"So far it hasn't attracted much attention."

"But it will."

"Yes, so I am afraid," agreed De Bono. His thoughts were troubled. He had heard that note in Grima's voice he did not like. He knew as well as Grima himself where Grima's political sympathies lay. Nothing was ever said between them but he was sharp as well as sensitive. He had let Grima brandish his newspaper under his nose in wry silence. So far they had worked together harmoniously without politics entering into it. But he could see an occasion might arise when they would find themselves on opposite sides of the fence. He thought of it as a fence between them rather than a ditch as Grima did. A fence over which you would lean and shake hands. (Perhaps this was part of the English influence of which Grima silently complained.)

"I am your friend, Alfred Grima," he thought, "if you would only believe it. We are both Maltese . . ."

On the other hand, however much he was Alfred Grima's friend, if he was going into politics seriously then he must tread very, very carefully in the present case. If he didn't then he might end up reading in the newspapers that *he* and not the murderer was the villain.

"We must be careful, Grima," he said softly.

Grima did not answer and for a moment he thought he had already aroused the man's hostility, then he realised Grima had put down the telephone and was speaking to someone else.

Grima returned to the telephone; he sounded both puzzled and anxious.

"Dr. De Bono, I have something to report. The girl Rose Grech did not come home to her grandmother's house when she should have done. She hasn't been seen since she went off the morning after the murder."

"Soon after she was taken there, in other words . . . How did she leave? Do they know?"

"She caught a morning bus into Valletta."

"It looks as though she never meant to stay there." He was thinking fast. "If she went off freely then it may not be as bad as it looks. She may have hidden herself away for reasons of her own."

"I think it's bad whichever way you look at it," said Grima who could sometimes see more clearly than De Bono and who was not in any case predisposed to look on the bright side.

"Who brought in this report? The grandmother?"

"No, not the grandmother," said Grima. "A young sister."

"I wonder why the grandmother didn't come herself?"

"Frightened of us," said Grima, putting his finger with accuracy more deadly than he knew on what was the truth. The whole Grech family were terrified, with the exception of Amelia.

Joe De Bono took a decision. "Grima," he said, "we need help."

"You've got your cousin, John Azzopardi," said Grima with as much irony as he ever allowed himself in dealing with the Inquisitor.

"Professional help," said De Bono significantly.

Grima stiffened at once. Eight years ago a policeman from London had been called in to help in a smuggling case. But eight years ago he, Alfred Grima, had not been a detective sergeant.

"That's not my decision to take," he said at once.

"Nor mine either," said De Bono, "but it is advice I must offer to the correct person." As he put down the receiver he said, with great sincerity: "Grima, pray that we are doing the right thing."

"I don't pray," said Grima aloud to the empty air. "At any rate not in the same language as yours."

In De Bono's office his typist covered her much abused machine, put on her jacket and teetered off home on her high heels. Six o'clock had come and it was time for the daily parade up Kingsway. Soon she was struggling gaily in the crowd of young people who surge into the main street every day at this time to jostle and talk and show themselves.

Rose Grech had once been among them.

Rose Grech lay on her back with her eyes wide open, her mouth was slack and she was breathing through it. Her throat and nose felt sore. Her legs and hands were not bound and she was free to move but she was too frightened. She was as much hobbled by her fears as she would have been by chains.

She lay there in the dark and did not even try to call out for help. It would have been no use anyway, no help would be forthcoming from behind those cold walls.

She put out a hand and touched the wall. It was rough and chilly; she was in a small, stone room of some sort. Even in the dark she could sense it was small. It was nothing more than a cell. The walls brooded over her. The ceiling was low.

There was also an earthy smell. Could the room be underground? Or was it just a very old disused room?

She formed the thought, so at once she wondered if "room" was quite the right word to use? Wasn't it really a prison? An old disused prison. She shuddered.

Beneath her was a mattress, she had a blanket over her, but at the moment she no longer felt cold, she felt raging hot. She was thirsty too. Slowly she sat up and drank from the cup of water by her bed. There was a plate of food there too but this she ignored. The water soothed her throat and she snuggled back into the blanket with a silent sense of comfort.

Almost unconsciously, certainly without clearly forming any thought in her mind, her hand went out and took the knife that rested on the plate. She ran her finger down the blade. Blunt. She slid it quietly under her pillow just as the door of her prison opened.

Although the door had opened, and opened wide to judge by the prolonged scratching noise it made, yet there was no more light in her prison. So it must be night. Night again, for surely it had been night when she arrived?

"It is always night in this place," she thought.

The door closed again, more quietly this time, and the person who had looked in on her had withdrawn again.

This happened several times over the next few hours. The quiet anonymous surveillance was very frightening to her.

The routine was always the same. The door opened quietly, someone stood there, approached a few steps and then went away. She began to pick out little details that went with the entrance. There was the sound of noisy breathing, then a faint rustle. Finally there was the smell of garlic, a smell usually so familiar as to go unnoticed, but now her nose was preternaturally sensitive.

After the last entrance she lay there thinking. The shock of the blow and her abduction had dulled her mind but underneath she was still an intelligent, observant girl. Now she was beginning to think again. And she could identify her captors.

She did not know where she was but she knew who she was with. Thoughts and memories began to flood back into her mind.

"They can't mean to kill *me*," she cried.

She began to shiver: where once she had been hot, now she was bitterly cold.

Joe De Bono offered a cigarette to John Azzopardi and tried to look urbane and worldly; it was not a part he was any good in; he was provincial and knew it.

"So you see if I mean to go into political life seriously this year I have to step carefully. It would be best if someone from outside took the responsibility for this case."

"Sergeant Grima isn't going into politics," pointed out John Azzopardi.

"Grima is always in politics. It's only the fact that he's a decent, good man that has prevented him being more of a worry to me than he has been so far."

"I see," John was thoughtful. "So were you thinking of me?"

"No." His cousin was regretful. "You are not substantial enough. You would not be accepted as a substitute for me."

"What did you have in mind?" He wondered what Joe was working up to, he had a part in it no doubt, or this conversation would not be taking place.

"I wondered about your London friend?"

"John Coffin?"

"Supposing I asked to have him sent out here? It has been done before."

"Supposing what? From what side are you expecting trouble? Are you asking me if John Coffin will be easy to work with? Or if he will be acceptable here? How can I tell?"

"I am asking you if he would be willing to come . . . ? His part would not perhaps be a noble one?"

"You mean you might want to muzzle him? He would never accept that."

"No." The Inquisitor was mildly reproving, even amused. "Muzzle! The word! What ideas you have. I am not corrupt. What is true must come out. Justice must not only be done, but must be seen to be done. A very sound political truth." His worldliness was not very convincing even to himself.

"And nothing is as unpopular and occasionally as expensive as justice?"

The Inquisitor sighed. "After all the English are used to being unpopular. And they don't really mind it. I believe they take it as a compliment. A testament to their probity."

"I think my friend John Coffin sometimes has enough

of unpopularity," said Azzopardi, thinking of John's lovely and spirited wife Patsy, and his difficult marriage.

Across the seas and under lowering dark skies (it was a wet night) a happy family were spending an unwonted evening all together.

"It has an hypnotic effect on me," said the father. "I mean I want to do it too. I don't think I could, though. Well, not for such a long time. My lungs and hearing aren't strong enough."

He listened for a little while. "Remarkable isn't it? I mean you don't even have to be in the same room."

"Some people have special little microphones and speakers fitted up so they can hear in the next room," said his wife in a detached voice.

"We don't need that," said the father proudly.

"We wouldn't need it in the next block."

"One thing is sure: whichever of our two professions it chooses it has the voice for it." He turned to his wife. "What about the new play? Tell me about the part you are offered."

John Coffin's wife was a successful actress. Her father, an actor but not a flourishing one, had given her the Christian name of Cleopatra which had been no help at all in either her private or professional life, giving people the wrong idea all round. She chose to be known as Patsy Partridge, when she wasn't Mrs. John Coffin, and under this name had become successful as an actress in comedy. But what with a late marriage and a strong desire to love and be loved, combined with an equally strong fear of showing it, a jealousy of Coffin's job and an uncertainty about her own, she was not always a comic character in the home. As a mother she wasn't sure whether she was going to be a joke or a disaster.

"It's Juliet."

"But aren't you a bit old for that?"

"Not really." She sounded amused. "The theme is not Shakespeare's Juliet and not Romeo's girl friend, but a Juliet of the deep, deep South who's aged about forty and looks sixty and is a nymphomaniac."

"Is it a comic part?" asked Coffin; he broke off. "My dear, should it cry like that?"

"I can't stop it. Don't listen. I don't."

"Ah, it has stopped now."

"No, it's only a lull. There, I knew."

"Well, it's strong, anyway."

"Yes, we've got it for life."

They started to laugh. The truth was they adored it, were hopelessly in its thrall, but they really hardly knew what to do with it.

Dead silence fell on the whole family, for a moment they were each cocooned in their happiness.

Then the telephone rang. It was typical of their life together that when they had settled into an equilibrium something should break it up. Coffin went to answer the telephone. When he returned he had a wry look on his face.

"I have an invitation to go abroad. Malta. A case. The boss says I have been asked for by name."

"Flattering."

"I hope so. My fans are more widespread than I'd realized. Anyway I can go if I want. But do I want? Yes, I suppose so."

"And leave your loving wife and family."

"You could come too," he sounded eager. "Do come, Patsy. I'd love that. Say yes."

"I can't leave the play. We're just going into rehearsals."

"Well, I can't take the baby on my own," said Coffin. "Do you hate me going? Would you rather I didn't go?"

"No. You are perfectly free to go."

"Oh, I'm free all right," said Coffin, but he sounded dissatisfied.

Patsy looked tense. "We're always look for *compulsions* in our relationship, you and I," she said with that didactic air which made her husband want to beat her. "I do it as much as you. I ask for an imperative from you. You can't give it and neither can I. I am free and so are you. Quite free."

"All right, so I'm free," said Coffin irritably. "So what?"

"So you'd better go to Malta and solve your case."

"All right then, I will," and he left the room, slamming the door behind him. "And I might not come back."

Cleopatra Patsy Juliet Partridge Coffin sat down on the sofa and burst into tears.

By this time it was raining too in Valletta with the rain and the wind sweeping in from the sea in gusts.

Amelia Grech was still in Mrs. Callus's flat. She had

made almost no comment on being told of the disappearance of her daughter. She had spoken very little all day. Mrs. Callus was nervous of her, and showed it. She herself looked pale and unwell as if she still felt the effects of yesterday's faint spell.

Presently Mrs. Callus served supper. "Your friend Olive called," she said as she poured the soup.

"I suppose she's had the police down there," said Amelia.

"I believe she has." Mrs. Callus was watching her unwanted guest as she ate. She did not eat herself. "She wanted to talk to you. However, you were asleep."

"Funny thing for me to be asleep during the day."

"It's the shock."

"No, but I've felt tired and sleepy *all* day. Here, you aren't drugging me?"

"No," said Mrs. Callus faintly.

"Wouldn't put it past you lot." Amelia drank her soup noisily.

Presently she said: "Where is my husband?"

"He is working, I think. He will be back soon, I expect."

"I expect you hope he will never be back?"

Mrs. Callus did not answer.

"You'll give him supper when he gets back?"

"I suppose so."

"You will." Satisfied with the effects she had made, Amelia went back to her supper. She was now eating *pasta* with meat sauce and hunks of crusty Maltese bread. She was a methodical careful eater, working her way through her food from one side of the plate to the other. There was little that was feminine about her movements but nothing graceless either. She was on too large a scale for the word feminine to apply; one might as well expect the maidens on the top of the Acropolis to be good at the waltz.

The other inhabitants of the big old house in St. Michael's Street came home and tried to take up their accustomed ways each night but it was not easy. They did not speak much and seemed to avoid each others' eyes.

That evening they drifted into Mrs. Callus's flat almost as if by agreement, or as if in response to some silent plea for support she was sending out. If Dr. De Bono had seen their behaviour he would have found in it some substantiation for his idea of a conspiracy. Not everyone was present. The girl Mary Colombo was not and neither was Michael Green. Mrs. Fenech stayed behind with her baby. The others sat together in Mrs. Callus's sitting-room; they badly needed a spokesman, but none came forward.

Eventually their presence penetrated even the state of dreamy somnolence into which Amelia Grech had sunk after her supper. She roused herself and stared at them like a sleepy Medusa.

"You looking for me," she said with an effort, and when no one answered, "You're looking at me, anyway." She seemed to have difficulty in rousing herself from her strange sleepiness. "You killed him and that's what I shall say as long as I live."

"The truth," began Peter Fenech.

"When the truth about what happened is known everyone will agree with me," cried Amelia.

"It isn't known yet," said Peter, with a spark of defiance.

"Don't you threaten me." Amelia stood up. She looked immensely strong and vital standing there but her power was as much from the force of her character as the strength of her arm. The arm however was not to be underrated. She gave Peter a push that sent him backwards to the wall. Mrs. Callus helped him up.

"I don't trust any of you," said Amelia. "You're all working away behind my back. But you can trust me; I mean what I say; I will protect myself." She showed them her arm with the muscles tense. "An eye for an eye, if I have to."

"I think you'd better all go away," said Mrs. Callus, almost in tears. Her neat sitting-room was taking on a disordered battered air. "I wish you could take her with you, but you can't." A chair fell to the ground. Amelia staggered against the table as if she was drunk. "You've drugged me." She once again repeated her accusation, her voice thick.

They looked at her in horror.

"Drugged," she said again. "Poison."

The Second Inquisition

VI

On the flight over John Coffin found himself sitting next to a decorative young man wearing dark glasses and reading a guide-book on Malta. On the table in front of him was a book called *Megalithic Malta*, another called *Malta and the Knights*, and a third called *Malta and the Mediterranean*. Coffin was impressed with such industry. He had his own homework in the case on his lap: notes taken on a long telephone call from John Azzopardi the night before. He was already forming his own ideas of the case and what had happened in the house in St. Michael's Street, Valletta. But he must first see how his ideas measured up to reality. He needed to see the place and the people. In particular he looked forward to meeting Dr. Joseph De Bono. He hummed happily. Life had taken a pleasant turn: he had discovered that by giving Patsy a sharp shock he could produce pleasantness in the home. They had parted on the best of terms and kisses all round, including the baby.

"I'm hoping to do a programme on Malta," confided the young man shyly, removing his dark glasses and ordering some brandy from the steward. "A short film you know, it's part of a series." Throughout their acquaintanceship he talked often of "the series" but Coffin never found out exactly what it meant or what other things were lined up in his series.

"For the B.B.C.?" Coffin was impressed.

"Oh no, I don't work for Aunty. I did start off with her, but I suppose I'm just not a natural-born nephew. No, now I free lance."

"And that works better?" Coffin was always interested by insights into other people's lives. This one looked particularly interesting.

"When it works at all it works splendidly. But there are lean periods. Undoubtedly there are lean periods." He was thoughtful.

"Not one at the moment," thought Coffin, noting the thick suède shoes and matching jacket and the crocodile spectacle case with gold initials.

"Is this series your own?"

"Oh no, I'm just joining in. The rest of my team fly out tomorrow. The idea for this was my own." He sank back into his seat and got on with his reading. So did Coffin.

Soon the young man leaned forward. "I read they've had an interesting murder in Malta."

"Murders aren't interesting. Messy and sordid, yes, not really interesting."

"They are to the outsider, but you're on the inside, aren't you?" He smiled at Coffin. "I recognise you. I had a few shots of you once when I was doing a film of crime in South London. You were walking along a road in Southwark as fast as you could go and talking to yourself. Made quite a dramatic shot it did."

"I never knew I was on television," said Coffin, fascinated and delighted.

"You weren't. The viewers never got to see that film."

"One of the lean periods then?"

"The very leanest. I was earning so little I could even pay my income tax."

First Sicily, then Malta slid into view beneath them, the plane sank in the air and landed on Luqa airfield. They sat waiting. Then the stewardess came towards Coffin, looked surprised and impressed.

"Would you please come first, Inspector Coffin? There is a car waiting for you."

So Coffin, tightly buttoned up in his new overcoat and bright-eyed and cheerful, stepped from the plane with an air of pleased expectancy that John Azzopardi, who had got very fond of him in London, found touching.

The second inquisition, taking place under the stress of the search for Rose Grech, was conducted in a different way from the first. Azzopardi, Coffin, De Bono and Grima were all present. This time they sat in a tight half circle around a table, rather as if they were interviewing the chap for a job, thought Azzopardi, and on a shelf behind them Coffin had a tape-recorder going. Grima had taken the whole thing well and merely looked resigned. He did not resent Coffin. Further, he had made a quiet but definite attempt to form a front with Coffin against

De Bono. Coffin himself seemed inclined to be sympathetic to Grima and keep a wary watch on De Bono. Perhaps he could not help feeling more at ease with a policeman, even one who spoke Maltese (in fact Grima spoke excellent English also, as his job required him to do), than with a lawyer, even although he spoke English. To John Azzopardi's eyes his friend seemed older and more subdued in these new surroundings than he had expected. Perhaps he was deliberately playing himself down.

The pattern of the questioning was also different.

Only two people were sitting in the room outside: Olive Feltcher and Mary Colombo. They were not looking at each other. Olive was humming and fidgeting away to herself, making little comments as if she was her own audience. At intervals she got up and moved to another seat in the room.

"That's a strange girl. Sitting there crying. I must mend this skirt. My stockings too." She shifted round the room, still was not satisfied and moved on again.

"Anyway, I can see that picture better from here, I wanted to get a good look at it. You need spectacles, Olive. Spectacles, spectacles." She broke into a little tune the burden of which was still that Olive needed spectacles. Mary Colombo wondered if she was doing it all on purpose. She knew Olive well by sight and had been told by her older sister never to speak to her. Other people had the same feeling of unease about Olive. She believed Olive knew and resented it.

"I don't like you, Olive Feltcher," said Mary to herself.

"Silly girl, silly girl," thought Olive, adding those words to her song which never rose above a monody. She must use telepathy. Or perhaps she could read lips. But she could not, however, read English and she pored over a newspaper she had found lying on one of the chairs, moving her finger along the line in a manner to suggest she did indeed need spectacles, and strong ones at that. She saw Mary, however, and the girl turned away from her glance. Olive had a fierce glint to her eye when she chose to use it.

Sergeant Grima came out himself to summon Olive, who trotted in obediently after him like a little dog that obeyed but wouldn't hesitate to slip away either if it got the chance. And perhaps give a nip to a heel too.

She gave a polite nod to Joe De Bono, ignored John Azzopardi and then met Coffin's eye.

"Another one," she muttered, and crossed herself hurriedly.

"Another one?" asked Coffin.

"She means you have the evil eye," explained Grima. "I'm the other one."

"She's a pretty rum-looking character herself," said Coffin. This morning Olive was wearing a very long, very old black coat which was two sizes too broad for her and sagged on the shoulders. To Coffin it looked like a nurse's top coat with all the badges removed.

"Oh, she's not as bad as she looks," murmured Grima tolerantly; he had room for Olive in his world.

"Where does she live?" Coffin was squinting down at the papers before him. "Harry's Bar? She own it?"

"Manages it. It's owned by a man from Sliema. But he never comes near it except to collect what money there is. Olive's got a bad reputation locally on account of managing the bar, but there's nothing in it. It's about the only job she could do, and she must live. She's done it for years now. I don't say she could have done it in the old days when all the bars along the water-front and down The Gut were crowded, but now, why there's hardly a soul goes in it."

"And that's where she lives?"

"Above it. In one room. Neat and tidy enough, but she's got everything there. I was with her once and she brought out a newspaper printed in 1939. Full of stuff about Mussolini it was. Said she kept it for the pictures."

"Strange friend for Amelia Grech." (Coffin had not questioned Amelia but he had read carefully her statement and the answers she had given to the questions asked. He had also taken the opportunity to observe her without her knowing. From John Azzopardi's window he had watched her tall, slightly masculine figure setting out with a shopping bag. She was moving slowly, her hand resting on the shoulder of her husband who seemed to give slightly beneath her weight. Coffin frowned as he watched her. "She walks like there's something wrong with her," he had summed up.)

"No, not really. They would both find it difficult to fall in with other friends."

Two fringe characters, decided Coffin, looking at Olive Feltcher's face. Perhaps it could have done with more of a wash this morning. Olive turned her face slightly and seemed to prefer not to look at Coffin. Joe De Bono's face did not offer her much comfort either, and she settled for John Azzopardi, fixing her eyes on his face with a steadiness that embarrassed him.

"Have said all once," she said, in her fluent but imperfect English. She usually spoke in Maltese, but the flick of a quick glance to Grima suggested that it was a show of defiance. In her long life Olive Feltcher had learnt many little underhand ways of asserting her independence; slyness had grown on her with the years so that the little girl who had danced in the sunshine by the Grand Harbour had grown into the withered woman who lived in the overcrowded room above Harry's Bar.

"We have to ask you again," said Dr. De Bono courteously. "Particularly address yourself to this gentleman, if you will," and he nodded towards Coffin.

In their discussion late into the night all four men had agreed that Mary Colombo must be questioned again. But Coffin had seen at once that Olive Feltcher was a decisive witness.

"She pinpoints the timing of the whole thing. I wonder you haven't hammered away at her. There she is in close contact with Amelia Grech while the boy is being killed and then she accompanies the mother home, or thereabouts. She knows when Amelia arrived, how long she stayed, and when they both went home. I know you say she's as difficult to get things out of as Amelia Grech herself, but she's in a much weaker position, *she* isn't the mother, *she* can be pressed. I think it's quite likely Amelia was out of the house much longer than she admits to . . .

She may even have cleared out on purpose. No, I don't mean she cleared out and left the boy to be killed, but there's something odd about that excursion of hers and I want to know what it is. If we can't get it from Amelia Grech then we must try Olive Feltcher."

"Miss Feltcher," he began.

"Miss Feltcher," repeated Olive, receiving the title with pleasure and repeating it. "Yes, I am Miss Feltcher." She assumed a more dignified look, no longer Olive but Miss Feltcher.

"Amelia Grech was with you on the night her son was murdered. Yes, I know you have said this. She came when?"

"Nine o'clock, nine-thirty," said Olive. "About that time. I have the wireless on. Switch B. Playing records."

"Rediffusion," put in Grima. "We've checked the times. She is right. The record programme ended at nine-thirty."

"My best programme," said Olive. "Lovely music. All singing."

"And you and Amelia Grech sat there talking and drinking until when?" asked Coffin.

"Not much talking, not much drinking, more just sitting."

A bright evening, thought Coffin. "Anyone else there with you?"

Olive shook her head.

"Business slack, eh?"

"Crowds now," said Olive happily; she seemed to have

settled down with Coffin and forgotten about the evil eye. "All come."

"Did Mrs. Grech come and sit with you often?"

Olive shrugged.

"What does that mean?"

"As it suited her."

"I don't think you like Mrs. Grech, do you?" said Coffin; there was an ominous crackle of vitality showing now in his voice and manner. "So he *was* holding himself in," thought John Azzopardi.

Olive did not answer.

"What have you got against her?"

"She liked a free drink."

"I've heard people call you friends. I don't believe you were friends."

Olive moved her head uneasily. "Not true. Did like Amelia before," she stopped and did not continue.

"Before what? Before the murder?"

Again Olive gave that little toss to her head as if trying to shake her brain clear of something.

"Before she married again," she said finally. "Got difficult then."

"Difficult? How?" Coffin looked at her. "Perhaps I should say: difficult with whom?"

"Boy. Husband. Everyone." Olive left it with him: he could choose.

"Over the boy?" It was Joe De Bono who put in this question. "He was a wild boy, wasn't he? He was the one who made things difficult?"

"You're right there," said Coffin, "but let her say it."

Olive sighed. "Ask Michael Green. He and the boy Hector," and she put her two fingers together side by side.

"As close as that?" said Coffin. He looked at De Bono as if to say: see where we're getting. "And Amelia Grech didn't like it?"

"Amelia didn't like it," repeated Olive. All three of her listeners felt that she got pleasure from saying it. And then hurriedly, "I don't want to get Michael into trouble."

"You won't get him into trouble," said John Azzopardi quickly: he had liked Michael Green about whom there hung an innocent sweetness, and he wanted to reassure this other crazy old innocent. But at the same time he remembered that he had always felt Michael and Hector must have been dangerous friends. There had been, somehow or other, an inflammatory quality to that relationship.

"Are you so sure?" said Coffin softly. "Well, you know your world best. I wouldn't be so sure myself."

"I am not," said Joe De Bono in measured syllables.

Grima kept silent. Possibly he was thinking that the finger-print of Mary Colombo had still to be explained.

"And was Amelia Grech especially angry that night when she visited you?" asked Coffin. "Was she angry with Michael Green? Had there been a quarrel? Is that why she came down here?" He pressed her: "Is that what you mean by suggesting we ask Michael Green?"

"She didn't say," said Olive; her loquacity was drying up again.

"Did Amelia come down here to get away from something in the house?" asked Coffin. "Had there been a quarrel between her and Michael Green about the boy Hector? Was there a quarrel in the house that night? Wasn't there?"

"Don't know," said Olive, sullenness settling down on her.

"You say you like Amelia Grech. Why are you so reluctant to tell us anything?"

He had put his finger on the crux.

Olive stared at him without trying to reply. She looked very frightened.

Her sleeve fell back from her right arm. There were three small but clear bruises on it like a bracelet.

"You were right then," said De Bono in a tired voice. "She knew something. She told us about Michael Green."

Coffin looked triumphant. John Azzopardi wondered if he himself looked as uneasy as he felt.

"She knows more, too," said the man from London. "We shall get it in time."

"If she isn't dead first," said John Azzopardi.

They all stared at him. It was an extraordinary thing to say and he felt it himself but the words had burst forth unpremeditated.

"Do you suggest suicide?" questioned De Bono.

"Murder," said John Azzopardi. "She's frightened."

"Perhaps you are thinking of those bruises?" asked Grima.

"She knows something and she is frightened."

"They are all frightened," said Grima unexpectedly. "There is a truth and they all know it."

"I agree," said Coffin. The policeman from London and the policeman of Valletta found themselves united. "I don't know if I'd call it 'a truth' though, things never are, more a collection of truths. Truth is never single and yet never divisible either."

Grima did not answer, possibly not understanding the other man's rapid flow of London English or possibly through an innate empiricism which made him prefer a simple truth (which he could check) rather than Truth.

"That is not how lawyers think," said Joe De Bono, with a touch of the Inquisitorial manner returning.

"You have equity," pointed out Coffin.

"Oh, that comes in the sphere of justice, which is something else again."

"Joe's putting on that cynical act," said John Azzopardi.

"Oh, my cousin only believes in suppressing the truth," said De Bono tartly.

"Not for ever," said John Azzopardi, turning the other cheek. That episode still rankled, then. One day soon he might have to tell his cousin exactly what had been the confession of the man killed in the car crash. It wouldn't help anyone, but perhaps after all this time it wouldn't hurt anyone either. He was feeling surly himself this morning. His afternoon with Chloe Zarb had ended on a sour note.

"I spoilt everything," he told himself. "Or perhaps Chloe did. Anyway we did it between us."

After their visit to the Inquisitor's Town Palace, Chloe had taken him on a tour of the island. They had driven up to the sweet thyme-covered slopes where the ancient track marks which confuse and intrigue archaeologists showed clear in the winter sunlight. Where do they come from and where do they go? Who cut them and how were they made? No one knows. No one knows anything about them except that they are man-made and have their place in the long history of the island as an inhabited place. Perhaps they belong to the Bronze Age or perhaps they go back to neolithic Malta when the great megalithic temples which make Stonehenge look provincial (as indeed it was in the Stone Age world, the centre of which was certainly the Mediterranean) were being raised.

John Azzopardi got out of the car and sniffed the air scented with herbs. The country about him looked bare and severe.

"It's so austere," he said lovingly.

"And yet compared with Greece it's verdant and rich."

"You've been to Greece?"

"This year." She was picking the thyme and rubbing it between her fingers. "In the spring."

"You don't stay at home, Chloe." He was aware of being faintly censorious. It wasn't good enough for Chloe to wear London clothes and smell of *Jolie Madame*. Or if you did, then you shouldn't pretend you wore a martyr's crown. Unconsciously he felt that dark and shabby clothes would be more suitable for someone placed like Chloe. He had been prepared for Chloe to be bitterly unhappy; he was not prepared for Chloe to be openly making a good thing of her life. The words making the best of it passed through his mind and were dismissed. Making the best of it implied privation, not French scent and trips to Greece.

Chloe shrugged. "I'm better away. Things are easier all round if Bertie doesn't see too much of me. Easier for me, easier for him. There's nothing to keep me home. Besides I like to travel."

"The privileges of irresponsibility have never been so clearly demonstrated," said John.

Chloe dropped the thyme she was sniffing as if it was suddenly bitter.

"You should have stopped yourself saying that. It doesn't come well from you. You weren't idle in England." Alice De Bono could have told John that Chloe could always defend herself.

"Never mind about me in England."

"I remember now how we always did quarrel. You were always so selfish. It was the worst thing about you," said Chloe.

"Selfish!"

"Yes, selfish."

"I treasured the memory of you, Chloe," said Azzopardi, white and angry. "I felt you were absolutely apart. A rose, if that isn't too romantic and poetic a word. I knew you were unhappy, that a lot of criticism came your way, but I never joined in."

"Thank you," said Chloe coldly.

"To me you were someone set apart . . . And I've come back from England to find you absolutely trivial."

"Selfish," said Chloe dispassionately. "Just what I said. And stupid too."

She got back into the car and they drove back towards Valletta in a silence so cold that it burned.

They circled the Verdala palace, passed ancient Rabat and the old walled capital of Mdina, and drove across country, their route flanked by the majestic arches of Wignacourt's aqueduct: and then through Birkirara and Hamrun and the enormously thick stone bastions with which the Hospitallers girdled Floriana, and so up into the fortified city of Valetta where the great Auberges of the knights with their epic and evocative names, Aragon, Provence and Castile, line the streets.

Chloe stopped the car and opened the door for her passenger.

He got out without speaking and started to walk away.

"Bad manners as well," said Chloe, as she turned the car to drive away.

"Yes, Chloe was right," thought Azzopardi, coming back into the present. "We always did quarrel." He met his cousin Joe's eye and smiled. Joe did not smile back, possibly he saw no occasion for it. I've gone sour on my little island, thought John Azzopardi, And then into the vacuum created in his mind by this statement surged a powerful feeling whose warmth astounded him. "It's not anger I feel for Chloe, but love. The feeling I had for her never dried up but just went underground." Now it was like a great river welling out, and all that had happened in England seemed unreal and flimsy like a dream. He was dismayed at his own blindness and what now seemed his shallowness.

He hardly heard his cousin's words.

"The girl Rose Grech has now been missing since the morning after the murder of her brother. If she is not found soon we shall have to assume she is dead too and that what we must look for is a dead body."

"In London we should already be looking for a dead body," said Coffin in a quiet voice.

But Rose Grech was not dead. Nor did she intend to be found dead if she could help it. She was sitting on the edge of her bed and she was sharpening her dinner-knife on the rough wall.

She raised the knife to the wall and drew the edge unsteadily across it at an angle. She did it again and then again. Then she tried the edge with her thumb. It was ragged but sharp. A very nasty little weapon was on the way to being formed.

Rose sat back on her bed and rested her head in her hands. She was ragingly hot and her throat ached. Her head no longer throbbed but it seemed to belong to a different part of her body altogether. Sometimes it was sitting in the air just over her neck, although not precisely on it, and sometimes it was floating high in the air in one corner of the little room where she was imprisoned. When it was in the corner in mid-air she could look down on her body and see herself lying there as if asleep, complete, oddly enough, with head.

"That's my *other* head," she remembered her voice saying hoarsely.

Her two heads were firmly welded together at the moment and both were sitting on her hands feeling almost as separated from her body as her brother's had been.

She went back to sharpening her knife and her head floated comfortably off to the ceiling, apparently abandoning her for ever.

"Tell the truth," she had urged poor Mary Colombo, but she had not understood how dangerous the truth really was and how much she herself was in the power of those who wanted the truth shut up and buried with Hector. And indeed, for all the brutality of Hector's death, she had not expected danger for herself.

She could see that Mary Colombo, the Fenechs, even Mrs. Callus were in danger, but she thought Rose Grech was protected. She understood better now, and even saw dimly that what could kill her, as it had already killed Hector, was not hate or malevolence, but anger and fear and stupidity.

She saw all this, but then she was the cleverest of all the Grech family.

"I'm not going to die," she muttered, licking hot and fever-encrusted lips.

She had no idea that she was dangerously ill.

Olive Feltcher had to pass Mary Colombo as she left Dr. De Bono. Mary was not alone any longer, for Dr. De Bono's secretary and a young policeman were gossiping in one corner of the room.

"I don't think I shall be working here much longer. It's so quiet. No life. I'm trying for a job at Rediffusion House."

"More life up there?"

"So exciting." She sighed. "People coming and going. People from outside. Do you know I've never even been to Italy? Sicily only and then it was in Lent."

"I've never been farther than Gozo."

"I've got a nice voice. They might even let me broadcast . . . and when television really gets going . . ." She sank so far into her dream that she couldn't even finish the sentence. Then she sighed. "There's nothing for a girl to do here, except be secretary in something very respectable and approved of and then get married and have kids. And I have ambitions. I wish I could go to Italy. I wish I could just go."

"Go then."

"And do what? I don't even type very well." She gave the machine a bang.

"I know that. I've heard you." He was a serious young man and took everything, even typewriters and pretty girls seriously. She *was* pretty though, with large dark eyes and shining hair and a golden skin.

"Dr. De Bono only puts up with me because he's a friend of my father's. I have no qualifications. I do nothing very well. Rediffusion is just a pipe-dream. I wanted to go to the university and study to be a doctor but my father wouldn't let me. He said I'd only get married."

"You should take notice of what your father says."

"Oh, I should?" She gave him a sidelong glance from

under her long eyelashes. "Well, I can tell you that one of the things he'd say to me is not to talk to *you*." She giggled.

The young policeman flushed.

They were so occupied with each other, with the paired dance that they were just beginning and which for them might or might not end in marriage (a young policeman was hardly a good match for a rich man's daughter) that they did not notice Olive go over to Mary Colombo. Nor did they hear what she said.

She waddled over to Mary, impeded by her big coat.

"They're getting close. I should tell the truth if I were you. You lot can't hope to keep it quiet much longer, now can you?"

"I don't know what you're talking about."

"I thought you looked a silly girl," said Olive with spirit. "I *know* what happened that night. Everyone must know by now. *They* don't know," and she jerked her heard towards the other room, "but they will soon. Even the police can't go on not noticing what's under their noses for ever."

She started towards the door.

"Tell the truth."

The advice was the same as Rose Grech had given and Mary Colombo received it as silently. But she had already told some of the truth to Dr. De Bono; little by little, it would be squeezed out of her. The process which had already begun would be continued.

She had told the police she had seen someone coming

out of the window of the Grech flat and trying to get down to the street below.

She had not, however, told the police who this person was, nor that in fact the figure had never succeeded in reaching the street. She had not told the truth about where she was herself when she saw this figure.

These were among the truths she suspected were about to be squeezed from her.

She moved quietly to the door, wondering if she could edge out of the room, escape and never come back. She even thought, although only briefly – she was not the suicidal type – of jumping from the upper Barracca Gardens down into the great ditch which had once been a moat around Valletta.

The young policeman looked up before she got to the door and smiled reassuringly before going back to his own conversation. He could acknowledge one pretty girl even while responding to another.

Checked, Mary turned back to her seat. Any minute now the door to Dr. De Bono's office would open and she would go in to have a little more of the truth squeezed out of her – the tooth-paste from the tube.

There were so many things hidden from the police. The true set-up in the Grech family (although Olive had helped them to a little knowledge on that score); the effect of this on the whole household of people in St. Michael's Street (although they had been given many indications); the reason why Rose Grech had been abducted (although the reason derived from the other factors).

Nor did they know of the question which had arisen in John Azzopardi's mind in the Palace of the Inquisitor in Vittoriosa when he looked at the prison. He himself remembered the question but did not yet grasp what had created it. Soon he would realise. It wasn't such a subtle point after all. Just a little matter of behaviour.

The door opened and Sergeant Grima beckoned to Mary Colombo. She went forward with the frightened, virtuous face of someone prepared to tell the truth but not all of it.

As she looked at them she was uneasily aware that she was not clever and that it was hard to tell convincing lies. The others had been wiser just to say they knew nothing. Was it too late for her?

"I don't know anything," she said experimentally. Dr. De Bono, who had a kind, wise face, looked at her so sympathetically that it was only with difficulty that she stopped herself rushing forward, seizing his hand and saying, "Look after me, sir, only look after me and I'll tell everything. Only I don't want to die."

"My poor child," he said, but with a hint of sternness. "Tell the truth."

This repeated admonition on all sides to tell the truth was unnerving. Mary Colombo had no great respect for the truth as such, she usually told the truth because it was easier and because she liked to keep in well with her parish priest. Too many lies admitted to too often in confession might produce uncomfortable penances. She was already doing penance for spraying herself lavishly with French scent from the dressing-table of an employer.

Father Vella had not been very censorious: he well understood the temptation offered by that rich gleaming liquid. He had pointed out that it was not only the theft but the *immodesty*! A pity she had had to tell him, Mary reflected, but the smell had been very powerful and Father Vella (who must have had a very worldly youth) had proved to know the smell of *Shalimar* by Guerlain as well as anyone. She could almost swear he had enjoyed the smell even while reproving her. She had certainly enjoyed it herself and it had been well worth getting up early and polishing the parish silver three mornings last week, especially as she had overslept twice, which couldn't be called a sin or her fault but just nature.

Thus propping up her conviction of her own uprightness, Mary was able to bite back the words which rose to her lips and which were: let me go home.

"Ah now, you'll tell the truth, won't you, Mary?" said Sergeant Grima. Mary found him even more alarming than the other man, the quiet one in the dark suit whom she had been studying out of the corner of her eye, so she just crossed her ankles and folded her hands in her lap, as she had been taught to do at school, and said nothing.

"I have read what you told the sergeant about seeing a figure climbing out of Mrs. Grech's window on the night of the murder," began Coffin. "It was the living-room window, of course? Not the bedroom where the boy was found lying?"

"No, you can't see that from the front."

"Do you know that you are the only person in the house or the street for that matter who admits to seeing anything?" He sounded interested but not surprised. Dimly she was aware that this man was infinitely more experienced than either of the two men who had questioned her before. There were worlds of wickedness and crimes of which she was ignorant but in which he was wise.

"I was the only one who saw," she agreed, thankful to be able to offer even this small piece of truth.

"And where were you when you saw it?"

"In my bedroom. I said that."

"And did you recognise the figure?"

"No."

"I think you did."

"Tell the truth," advised De Bono.

'She'd better," said Grima. He was looking grim. "Do you want to go the way of Rose Grech? She's missing, you know."

Tears began to appear in Mary Colombo's eyes, which already looked red and sore. She dabbed at them with a coloured handkerchief.

"Ah, don't bully her," said John Azzopardi, thinking he had never seen the girl without tears in her eyes. "She's been bullied enough already, I think, and not by you." He frowned at her. "Who were you hiding from that night I found you hiding, Mary? Was it Hector? Were you frightened of him physically?"

Tears were welling from her eyes now in great streams, tears of fear and weakness, and even, in a curious sort of way, of relief, that some of her terrible burden was being dragged from her.

She shook her head wordlessly but in a way that carried conviction. "No, not Hector. Nice boy," she said eventually.

"That's the first time I've heard him called that," said Grima.

"Who was it you saw coming out of the window?" said De Bono in a quiet but determined voice.

"I don't know."

"Perhaps there was never anyone at all," he said softly. "Perhaps you invented him?"

"No, no, I did see him, but . . ." she stopped. She was so caught up in the half-lie she had told it was difficult for her now to work out what she had to say. She put a hand up to her face unsteadily.

"We have your finger-print, Mary," said De Bono in an even quieter voice, so soft that the hum of the tape-recorder in the background could be heard. "And from the circumstances of its finding we know it must have been made that night. So you see we *know* you were there in the room with the murdered boy."

The tears dried up and Mary Colombo miraculously regained courage. "I didn't kill him, no I didn't."

"So. What about the print?" said De Bono sceptically.

"I admit now that I was in the room. I came down when I thought I heard a noise. I came into the room." She was breathing quickly and nervously, her words tripping over each other on her tongue. "I was curious. I came in, I must have touched something, then I saw *him*." She shuddered.

"What did you see?"

"I saw Hector lying on the floor. In the room where they lived. I could tell he was dead from the way he was lying. He was lying there on the floor as he had been killed."

One truth about Hector Grech's death. London or Valletta it was all the same, thought Coffin. You pressed them hard enough and one little bit of the truth came out. You leaned on them harder, making it really hurt and the rest came out. All killers always thought they could get away with it for ever and ever amen, until you showed them otherwise. When you got down to essentials the Grech murder case was the same as a dozen others that had faced him in London. He thought the motive, which he was beginning to believe he understood, the same mixture of the trivial impulse and deep-rooted emotions. The decapitation of Hector Grech was a puzzling and macabre feature, but even for this he was beginning to see a motive.

If Mary Colombo was telling the truth she had seen the body lying on the floor of the living-room. He had been found by his mother lying on the bed in her room. There were also signs of blood in the kitchen. So the body had been moved once and possibly twice.

Joe De Bono, Coffin and Sergeant Grima had a muttered, quiet consultation. Mary Colombo looked on anxiously as John Azzopardi made his contribution. She thought she caught one word: falsity, and shifted uneasily in her seat. She was well aware that they were a quartette that promised no good to her.

She could tell from the way De Bono put his papers on

the table that the interview was nearly over and tried to tell herself that it had gone well. Then she saw that Coffin was not finished.

"There's one other death I'm interested in, someone else died just about when Hector Grech did; perhaps it's coincidence, perhaps it's not. A bird died. Do you know anything about that?"

The question was unexpected; she was off her guard.

"Oh, the bird was dead before that," said Mary Colombo.

"*Was* it?" Coffin sat back. "I'm like a mole. I work away underground making little tunnels through the ground, more or less blindly, just as the lie of the land dictates to me, so that eventually the ground will give beneath the liar's feet. But I can't predict exactly when and how it will go. To drop the metaphor, as a questioner I can never be quite sure exactly which question will do the trick. Whether she knows it or not the ground has now broken up beneath her. She has let me know exactly how much and what sort of thing she is holding back."

He met Dr. De Bono's eyes and there too he saw the knowledge that the girl had revealed herself. She still knew a great deal more than she had told them. Grima understood it too. Only John Azzopardi seemed unaware. Coffin shook his head slightly at De Bono: no, no more yet. We won't press.

But Mary Colombo blundered on. "That was why Hector was in such a state that night. His bird was dead and he thought Michael would mind." Coffin watched and listened, fascinated; you hardly had to help her at all, she couldn't stop the words coming out. So great was her wish to tell and so painful the suppression forced upon her that now she had started she couldn't put the brake on. This strong desire of witnesses to void the truth is what all policemen play upon; its basis is hardly a reverence for truth, not always even guilt, but a need to relieve the speaker. But when it starts to operate the process is never pretty. "Oh, Hector was wild. We all knew it, he could hardly be kept in at all. Screams . . ."

"Did someone kill the bird?" interrupted Coffin.

"Oh no, no, I don't think so. It died naturally. Amelia forgot to feed it."

"Naturally," commented Coffin. "Amelia always forgetful?"

"She wouldn't bother much about a bird."

"But Hector did?"

"Oh yes, Hector did," her words were slowing down now. Coffin saw that she was beginning to see she had opened Pandora's box. She could hear the sound of the evils flying round her head. Hope was still at the bottom of the box but she hadn't started to look for it yet.

"And Michael Green? He minded?"

She didn't answer this at all. The noises round her head were louder.

"And there's one other thing. You say you were safely in your own room with your sister that night?"

Mary Colombo nodded.

"And now you tell us you went downstairs to investigate and actually went into the room?"

The furies were howling round Mary Colombo's head now.

"But *why* did you go in and look? You're a nervous, timid girl, surely it's not the way you usually behave? Why did you go and look? Tell me that."

Mary Colombo did not answer; she looked sick and frightened.

"A very faulty little story," said the Inquisitor when she had gone. "I would have pressed her if you had given me the chance. But perhaps you were right. Yes, perhaps you were right."

"When we know *why* she went into the room we shall know the murderer," said Coffin. "It wasn't bravery that took her in there."

"Curiosity?" said Grima.

Coffin shook his head. "Not that girl. Michael Green put his head under the pillow, and the rest of them tried to do more or less the same. Mrs. Callus turned her music up louder. No, Mary Colombo wasn't the only brave one. If she went to look then she went because she had to. Something made her."

"I don't believe Michael Green would kill a boy, his friend, because of a bird," said John Azzopardi, much troubled.

"No. Nobody would. It's simpler and more natural than that. You could call this one of the most natural murders in the world." "Azzopardi does not appreciate the situation at all," thought Coffin, but he knew that Grima and De Bono must do so.

"We have to see Michael Green; we have to find the girl Rose Grech."

"She knows something?"

"No more than they all know. I think they all know what happened when Hector Grech died. What is quite clear is that Rose Grech amongst them wanted to tell the truth. She has been prevented."

The entrance of Michael Green did not take place as expected. The policeman sent to his place of work to collect him reported that he had not been seen there all day. Nor had he gone to work the day before. He had not been seen for two days by his superior, who was beginning to get restive.

"This is the sort of thing you are supposed to know," said De Bono angrily to Grima.

Grima muttered something about it not having been reported.

"You don't wait for things to be reported; you find out," said De Bono icily. He was all Inquisitor now. The two men were close to quarrelling. Grima was beginning to look both hurt and sullen, a dangerous combination of emotions.

"I've had all my available men out looking for Rose Grech," muttered Grima.

The interchange was in Maltese so Coffin could not follow the words, but he could read their faces.

"This man has not been at work for two days. No one has seen him and we have to be told." De Bono banged his hand on the table in a florid gesture.

"I think we ought to go round to where he lives in St. Michael's Street," Coffin spoke.

"And see the people there?" went on De Bono angrily. "I suppose this will be one more secret they have been keeping."

"Very likely," said Coffin, and then changed his mind. "No, on reflection, I think not."

"Could he be wherever Rose Grech is?" asked John Azzopardi.

Coffin shook his head silently. "Let's go, shall we?"

"We shall have to walk," said De Bono with a groan. "You have to circle half Valletta to do it with a car." He hurried down the stairs and out into the street. The others followed, each in his own way reflecting the tension of the moment.

Alice De Bono watched them go from an upstairs window. "They look like it's the end of the world." She laughed and went back to her sewing. She was sewing a short white dress of cotton and smocking it delicately. She had seen her husband greet the end of the world too often to feel real anxiety. "He flies off the handle. Grima's going to hit him one day." But comfortable in the knowledge that Grima would never in fact hit anyone and that his reputation for toughness was entirely due to the story that as a boy he had fallen from the Upper Barracca and survived, she went back to her sewing. The story was almost certainly false; the Upper Barracca is three hundred feet high and no one could survive such a fall, not even Alfred Grima. She had never found Grima alarming.

"You've got a man on duty there?" Coffin spoke to Grima as they hurried down the sloped street, slippery with rain.

"Had one ever since the murder."

"So if he has reported nothing, then nothing obvious has happened there." Coffin was thinking aloud. Grima kept quiet. He knew that the policeman on duty at St. Michael's Street was not the brightest of his boys nor gifted with acute powers of observation. He had been worrying over this quietly ever since he had heard that Michael Green was missing. If he was missing. There was more than one way of going missing, he mused unhappily.

The tall old house in St. Michael's Street had the same air of false, uneasy peace that it had always had. No one was about, not even the policeman, and Grima looked about him angrily. He shouted, raising reverberations in the quiet, dusty hall.

The policeman appeared from the back, chewing. "What's all the row?" he started to say, and stopped when he saw who it was. He swallowed his mouthful hastily. "Just having some coffee."

"Have you seen the man Green?"

"I haven't noticed." He scratched his head. "Not to remember."

"Would you notice anything?" Grima was more despairing than unkind. "Got the keys to his place?"

"I've got all the keys." He patted his pocket. "Mrs. Callus gave me them. She keeps duplicates all the time. But nothing's ever locked."

"This one might be," said Grima, taking the key and running up the stairs.

Michael Green lived behind a narrow green door that needed painting. Coffin tried the door; it was locked. He nodded to Grima who put the key in the door and turned it. The door still did not yield.

"Bolted on the inside," Grima spoke over his shoulder. "We know what we're looking for now, don't we?"

"At any rate we know what we shall find," Coffin corrected.

"Do you think the Grech girl is here too?" said De Bono, agitated.

Coffin shrugged. Grima was busy forcing the door.

The air inside the room was stale and stuffy; it smelt of kerosene and human beings. Green had two small rooms with a folding door between. The outer room was empty but the door to the inner room stood open.

Michael Green was lying curled up on the bed with one hand under his cheek. His face was swollen and red with a prickly, scattered rash on the cheeks and neck. He was wearing a clean white shirt and dark trousers.

There was a cup and saucer by the bed and propped against it was a sealed envelope addressed to Dr. De Bono.

Coffin handed the letter silently to De Bono, then picked up the cup. A thick sediment filled the bottom; he sniffed, put his forefinger in and then delicately licked it.

"Aspirin," he said. He sighed.

De Bono had been reading the letter. It began without preamble.

"So sorry. At first it seemed easy to bear – each day now is worse. I am sick, empty. Michael Green is dead now. I should have saved Hector who was my friend. I blame myself. The reason for killing Hector was anger. Poor Hector. It was my fault he got excited and wild. I thought I was a good friend but I was a bad one. He was hit in anger, that I know. I don't call it murder but I feel guilty. I am guilty. I have hidden the truth because I was frightened. But what fear is worse than . . . self . . . empty . . . I took three aspirin for my headache. Then three more. Accident really."

There were blots and what looked like tears. The letter did not end, it tailed off as if the writer had dropped asleep over it.

De Bono looked up. "I would never have believed it of him. Peter Fenech, perhaps, yes, this one no."

"You can believe it of anyone," said Coffin.

"But for us it is such a sin."

"He really believes that that could act as a check," thought Coffin, and then with surprise added to himself: for *him* it would be.

"It must have seemed such a little sin by that time," he said sadly, looking down on Michael Green, whom he now saw for the first time. "And at that, he tried to cover it up by pretending, perhaps even to himself, that he took the stuff by accident." He looked down at the stricken face. "He has far more than six aspirin inside him."

"Is this a confession of guilt of the murder of Hector Grech?" asked John Azzopardi, who had been reading the letter.

Coffin shook his head. "It doesn't say so."

"I don't think it is," said De Bono heavily, "which is what makes it all so terrible."

But Grima had been leaning over the bed, examining the body. Now he spoke urgently, "I think he is not dead. There is still some life." He had his hand under the shirt and on the bare chest over the heart. "I feel *something*."

He stood up. "We must get him to hospital." He and Coffin faced each other. "He has had the stuff inside him for over twenty-four hours. There is not much chance."

"Nearer thirty-six, I reckon." The two men were professionals now, ignoring Azzopardi and De Bono. "You get on to the hospital and I'll try what I can do in the way of artificial respiration." He was already taking off his coat and rolling up his sleeves, glad to be about the simple human task of resurrection.

VII

Amelia Grech was still staying with Mrs. Callus. They watched Michael Green being taken off to hospital together. Mrs. Callus was a reluctant audience, but Amelia was avidly interested.

"They've covered him up," she reported, "but not his face. So he's not dead. Not yet."

"Poor fellow." Mrs. Callus rubbed her hands together as if they were cold; perhaps they were, the weather was chilly and wet for Malta. No golden sun shone today, but steady heavy rain fell which London itself could not have bettered.

"One of my enemies gone," said Amelia Grech with satisfaction.

"You're mad." Mrs. Callus was sharp. "Poor fellow, he was no one's enemy, not even his own."

"Well, that's your way of looking at it," muttered Amelia, finding her customary difficulty in putting her feelings into lucid speech. Perhaps a lot of her trouble would never have arisen if she could have been more articulate. She slumped back in her chair, staring into her lap.

Mrs. Callus looked at her and was depressed by what she saw.

"You've done no work today, none since Hector was killed. Don't you think you ought to start again?" she suggested timidly.

"I am mourning," said Amelia. She raised her head. "None of *you* mourn Hector."

"Hector is dead now," began Mrs. Callus.

"Not buried yet, though," said Amelia. "Don't forget that. Not yet buried." Maltese funerals are usually held the day after the death, but in Hector's case the body had been retained for forensic purposes.

"I don't forget." Mrs. Callus looked as if she might faint. "You don't let me. Every day you describe Hector's body to me: how he died, how he was lying. The blood, his eyes, his tears. You tell me all. It wasn't my fault. It wasn't I that killed him."

"You all hated Hector," said Amelia standing up. "Just as you all hate me. I know you." She towered above her landlady. "I believe you did try to poison me. *Something* has happened to me, I know, I don't feel right."

"I'm frightened of you," whimpered Mrs. Callus, all trace of her old sophisticated manner gone. It would be difficult to say which woman had changed the most since the murder of Hector Grech and the beginning of Amelia's symbiotic existence on Mrs. Callus. On the whole Amelia's character seemed to have stood up to it best. She remained herself, although somewhat changed physically: she was slower and clumsier. As to her hostess, a few more days of Amelia, one would have said, and

Mrs. Callus would disintegrate altogether. This was partly because of the unending stress of task and errands her guest subjected her to: she was already counting the days to Amelia's departure.

"Hated me. Made me feel unclean. Unwanted. Worse for Hector. Telling me – keep him quiet; stop him being a nuisance. No noise." Amelia was grumbling slowly on, "No noise, how I could stop him making a noise? How could I stop any of us making a noise?"

"You never did," said Mrs. Callus wearily.

"Human beings," countered Amelia, who was under no illusions that it was a battle she was fighting, and one to the death. It was them or her, was how she reasoned.

Mrs. Callus also knew that it was a death struggle. She blamed herself for not having more courage. The others are uneducated people, weak, defenceless, she told herself, but I ought to be able to speak to Grima, put our case, make him understand.

But she knew that she would not do this because she was deeply and physically afraid of Amelia Grech. Amelia had them all in thrall. She walked to the window and looked out with all the depression and self-pity of someone who is caught in a prison created by herself. She was too weak to get out and knew it, whereas Amelia, trapped in a similar prison, had shown rough courage in getting out of hers.

Amelia stirred. "Play me some music," she commanded. She had issued this order many times now. Mrs. Callus knew what it meant. Obediently she went over to the gramophone and put on a Tchaikowsky waltz.

Amelia drank in the rich, sensuous, self-pitying music.

"A little more," she said dreamily, "a little louder."

"What extraordinary taste she has," thought Mrs. Callus, as she complied; she did not consider Tchaikowsky great music. "But I suppose for a woman like her . . ." Even in this moment of her utter despair she could not refrain from passing a judgement.

"Now the one about the stabbing," said Amelia.

Mrs. Callus recognised what was wanted and put on *Tosca*.

Amelia lay back and gave herself up to the enjoyment of it. For the moment she was at peace: a magnificent, if now slightly maimed figure.

"Michael Green may live, there is a chance," said De Bono turning away from the telephone in his own office. "Resuscitation is still going on. He had vomited a lot of the aspirin apparently."

"I noticed that."

"Excuse me a moment," said De Bono disappearing and closing the door carefully behind him. They could hear him walk up the stairs.

"Gone to speak to his wife," said John Azzopardi to Coffin. "Alice is a cousin of mine."

"Who isn't?" asked Coffin.

Grima came into the room, frowning. "Where's Dr. De Bono?"

Azzopardi pointed upstairs.

"I've just got hold of Mary Colombo again. Told her we want to see her again. Brought her round with me now. We've got to get everything she knows out of her and fast."

"I don't think it'll take much doing."

"Nor me . . . She's frightened stiff. She told me that she thinks it was to see her that Rose Grech came into Valletta."

"What?"

"Yes. They met. Can you beat it? She's kept that to herself until now. Rose Grech started to speak to her, asked her to tell the truth or something."

"Excellent advice," said Coffin.

"She must be a good girl, this Rose Grech," said Grima sadly. "There they were, Rose and Mary, in St. Michael's Street (and I'll have a word with the man on duty there about this) and then someone came up, the girls got frightened and Mary ran off. She hasn't seen Rose since."

"Who was this someone?"

"Says she didn't see. She was frightened, so she covered her head with an apron and ran off."

"Is she telling the truth?"

Grima shrugged. It was a good shrug, thought Coffin, it combined "Who can say?" "She's a little liar," and "What is truth" all in one gesture.

De Bono came back looking more cheerful than when he had left.

"You are all to eat dinner here with us. My wife invites us. You too, Grima."

"Mrs. De Bono won't want me."

"Certainly she does." It was a ritual with them that

Grima should pretend to be not wanted and Joe De Bono should persuade him. In fact no one appreciated Alice De Bono's cooking more than Alfred Grima and the two were quite friends, often enjoying a joke over De Bono's unconscious head. Joe De Bono found it very hard to laugh at a joke even when it was explained to him.

"I'll be glad to, then." Grima did not attempt to hide his hunger and was first towards the door.

They filed upstairs past the family portraits that hung there to the large and sombre dining-room furnished in red velvet and damask. It was all handsome solid furniture, which had been specially built for the house a hundred years ago and which two wars had not shifted. When the house had been used as offices during the last war the furniture had been covered up and left. Alice De Bono thought it was probably impossible to move it by now.

The large table was covered with a white cloth and spread with food. Long loaves of crusty bread, a steaming dish of a thick white *pasta* with a meat sauce, a big bowl of salad and little tomatoes were placed at intervals. Three bottles of golden wine stood on a side table.

"Help yourselves," said De Bono, waving his hand. But Alice would have none of this and moved forward to serve her guests. Grima, attaching himself to her, carried round the food. Coffin found his mouth watering and started to eat the plain, good food hungrily.

"Two other guests are coming," said Alice De Bono with satisfaction. She smiled at her husband who raised his eyebrows in query. "Aunt Lily Louise and Chloe Zarb.

They have eaten but will join us in a little while for wine and coffee."

John Azzopardi, who had been enjoying his food, put down his fork and looked hard at his cousin Alice. She appeared innocent and probably was, but she was also Chloe Zarb's closest woman friend. So too was Baroness Castaldi, although she might also be called her closest critic as well, as so often happens between an older woman and a younger.

Chloe and Lily Louise Castaldi sailed in together looking sleek and well-dressed. Lily Louise's pearls were the biggest but Chloe had the brightest diamonds.

Coffin, susceptible as ever, hardly knew which woman to talk to first. Perhaps it was inevitable he should choose Baroness Castaldi, or perhaps Lily Louise Castaldi saw to it that the younger woman was directed to the same end of the table as John Azzopardi.

"I don't like people to quarrel, do you?" she said, turning her large brilliant eyes on Coffin.

"No, not much, that is, hardly ever. Well, I often quarrel with people myself." He was completely dazzled.

"Ah, not with people you are really fond of?"

"With them most of all," said Coffin sadly, thinking of his wife.

Across the table John Azzopardi had gone back to eating. Chloe was talking to Alice and Joe De Bono was looking serious. He did not like young women who said that their husbands had spent all their money to have such large diamonds. Yet he would have been the first to be angry if Chloe had sold the Zarb family jewellery. But family jewellery should be the old Maltese gold work such as his wife wore; Alice had thick yellow gold ear-rings and brooches worked in the Maltese way by local jewellers, and fine gold chains set with turquoises and aquamarines. *That* was what women should wear – not gaudy white stones dug up in Africa, polished in Amsterdam and then set in Paris. But in this he did Chloe an injustice: all her jewellery came from London.

Alice and Chloe were talking together in the low but audible voices of women who are only pretending to have a confidential conversation and are really quite happy to have people hear.

"So there you see," said Alice. "I will not, after all, go to England next spring. I shall be otherwise occupied."

Chloe laughed. "You won't ask me to be godmother?"

"So that's what it was all about," thought John Azzopardi. "There is to be another child and Alice was at first cross and is now pleased. And Joe?" He turned expectantly towards his cousin.

"You see how it is," said De Bono, half proud and half reluctant. "But I hardly know how to bring up and educate all my sons as it is!"

"Look on the bright side: it may be a daughter."

"So it might." De Bono looked pleased. "You know I never thought of that . . . If so, then we must have Chloe for godmother." Quite unconsciously his eyes fell upon the diamonds.

Chloe laughed.

The emergency meal was rapidly taking on the appearance of a celebration. Coffin was experienced enough as an investigator to recognise the occasion for what it was; the moment in the case when nerves and imaginations demonstrated their need for a rest. They had all tried very hard over the Grech case; here was their chance for relaxation and they were taking it. Such a moment came in almost every important case, a sort of detective's Walpurgis night when inhibitions were down. Strangely enough it seemed to come just when the case was about to fold up, as if the mind had run on ahead and already knew the answers.

John Azzopardi drained his glass of wine and turned to his cousin Joe. "Do you need me for the next few minutes?"

"No." The Inquisitor had his mouth full. Grima also was eating enthusiastically, breaking off pieces of crust and mopping them round his plate. "The Colombo girl can wait: she's kept us waiting."

"So she has," said Grima.

"Come out into the garden and look at Alice's orange-trees, Chloe?" asked John Azzopardi.

"It's raining," answered Chloe, not moving.

Alice leaned forward. "Oh no, it's stopped now. The moon is up."

"Well, not oranges then," said Chloe rising. "We'll walk towards the Upper Barracca, there's a nice little house up there that I want to have a look at."

"No, not Walpurgis Night," thought Coffin, watching them go out, "but All Fools' Night." He was conscious of having drunk a little too much wine.

"Thank you for giving me a chance to apologise," said John Azzopardi as he walked by Chloe's side.

"Oh? Is that what I'm doing? Then let's go back." Nevertheless, she walked on, even faster.

John trotted after her at a disadvantage, only able to see her back and a swathe of pale fur.

"Explanation, yes. Apology, no," she threw back.

"Explanations are harder."

Chloe did not answer. "There's the Manoel Theatre," she said nodding her head towards a side street. "It's been redecorated since you were away. Lovely, isn't it?"

The Manoel Theatre is the oldest and most elegant of eighteenth-century theatres still in use in Europe and Chloe's admiration was justified. Nevertheless it irritated John.

"Chloe, I believe you like buildings better than people."

"Certainly I do. Better than husband, better than cousins. Better than friends."

"You are bitter." He had caught up with her again.

She shrugged. "It's something to work at."

They were swept up in a throng of people coming out of a cinema, surging into an already crowded Kingsway. Voices and snatches of conversation rose all round them. "*Buona notte. Saqa.* Carry on," called a *karrozin* driver to his fare. "Let's go down the Gut," called one hopeful sailor to another. "They say it opens up at night." John Azzopardi found himself almost drawn into a conversation between a man he recognised as a local historian, a serious sober fellow, and another man in a suède jacket and matching shoes, whom Coffin could have told him was his companion of the aeroplane, the film producer from London. It was quite dark now but he was still wearing his dark glasses.

"Would you say it was the greatest man-made fortification in the world?" he was saying hopefully. He got no answer beyond a frown. "Well, till the Maginot Line, then?"

The historian was thoughtful and seemed reluctant to answer. "Could be. There's the Great Wall of China, of course. That would come to a huge area if you added it all up. Yes, I should say the Great Wall of China was the bigger." He sounded quite enthusiastic about the claims of the Great Wall of China.

"In Europe, then," said the man in suède, who seemed a little put out. "The biggest in Europe, would you say?"

"There's the Palace of Diocletian," said the historian with the air of one about to sum up impartially. "I think that must be nearly as big and that's fortified . . . No, I don't think there'd be much to choose between Valetta and Diocletian's Palace." He sounded satisfied that he had arrived at a fair judgement. "And then there's Hadrian's Wall in Britain," he said, his eyes kindling at the thought of more comparisons.

"Oh, hell. It's no good to me unless I can tell the viewers it's The Biggest."

The crowd parted them from Chloe and John Azzopardi.

"Honesty is always a tiresome companion," said Chloe wryly. She looked at the man by her side. "Isn't that really why you and I are taking this walk, John, because you are finding an attack of honesty uncomfortable? You feel you treated me badly, as you did, are honest enough to want to say so, and honest enough not to enjoy it."

"Yes, but, Chloe, there's so much more to say," began John.

"Then don't say it. A good many things are better left unsaid."

"You can be explicit enough yourself sometimes." In spite of himself he was getting irritable again: you took Chloe out under the cynical eye of your friend from London, you made ready to confess love and devotion and she started to cut you up with verbal knives. As he thought over what Chloe had said to him he began to think he had been wrong to call her "not clever". She might not be clever but she seemed to have an instinctive eye for placing a wound where it hurt. "Because she's been hurt pretty often herself," said an inner voice.

"Let me be explicit now, then: whatever you have have heard about me since you got back, some of it is true and some of it is not. This is a small place and there's always a focus for gossip. Last year it was the Admiral's wife; this year it's me. We both earned it. Now, shall we leave it at that?"

"No, but Chloe..."

"Don't create peace of mind for yourself by attacking mine," said Chloe, looking away. They were in the Upper Barracca Gardens now and from where they stood, she could see across the Grand Harbour to Vittoriosa and Senglea. "Because that's what you're after." She stared at the twinkling lights. "Bertie may be and is a drunken sot but he *is* my husband, and for us," there was a slight emphasis on the word, "there is no divorce."

"Would you divorce if you could, Chloe?"

"Yes, of course, what do you think I am? And I may come to it yet if I can travel much farther along the path I am on at the moment, but I haven't travelled it yet."

"Is that all the future holds for you, then? Travelling?" asked John sadly. He no longer grudged Chloe her pretty *ensembles*; they were only travelling clothes.

The damp, strong Gregale was blowing across the Harbour, whipping up the water. Rain was beginning to blow in their faces. It was time to go back.

"I only wanted to make-up friends, Chloe," said John Azzopardi, the old child-like words coming easily to his lips.

"No love? No hate?" She held out her hand.

"No. Just a good deal of affection and admiration."

They turned back, out of the darkness, across Castile Square now gleaming with rain, into the crowds of Kingsway.

"And what will you do?" asked Chloe. "Now you are back with us?"

There was comfort in the "us". "I really think that my first idea was my best," said John with resolution. "I shall settle down and have a career."

"I approve of that," Chloe sounded remarkably like the Baroness Castaldi. "I was quite right about her," was Azzopardi's reaction, "by the time she's Aunt Lily Louise's age she'll be a fierce *'grande dame'*."

He laughed. "I shall have to make my confession to Joe first. He is dogging me waiting for it and so is Grima."

"Your confession?"

"You know what it is; you must do if you've been anywhere near Joe De Bono in the last four years. He must mention it daily."

In the crowd, they passed the suède-jacketted figure still talking with animation to an increasingly gloomy companion. "No, it's not the smallest," he heard the historian say. "It might be the worst but it isn't the smallest." The search for the superlative was still going on.

"It's about the Kingsway robbery."

Five years ago twenty thousand pounds made up in three bundles had been stolen as it was being taken into the Airways Building. It was the largest sum that had ever been stolen in Malta and the thief, who had been masked, had shot two men, one fatally, and got away down an alley and never been seen again. Neither had the money. To this day it remained a mystery and one that rankled. The Valetta C.I.D. had bitter feelings about the case. A policeman working on the case had been accused of knowing too much and a question mark left hanging over his reputation. A certain man, an inhabitant of Rabat, had been suspected, but there had never been any evidence to convict him; later he committed suicide in despair. Or possibly, as the police maintained, because he was guilty. The same man's elderly uncle, an inhabitant of Mosta, was suspected of being an accomplice or, at the very least, of knowing about the theft and where the money was. He was watched for months, but without any evidence one way or another being discovered. This man had been caught in a car crash, near St. Paul's Bay, and been dragged from the blazing wreckage by John Azzopardi. They had been alone for about twenty minutes before help came, and the police maintained that during this time the dying man had made a full confession to the young lawyer. But, if so, John Azzopardi would never repeat it. Or even admit that it had been offered.

"So he did talk to you that night," said Chloe. "I always thought he must have done."

"Yes, of course, I suppose everyone knew it really. Perhaps I was wrong to keep quiet, Chloe, but he *asked* me . . ." He was silent for a minute as if thinking it out all over again. "He told me that his nephew was guilty, that they had planned the theft together, but that after his nephew killed himself, he destroyed the money. He himself had had nothing to do with the actual theft or the killing, but he had hidden the money. What was I to do, Chloe? By the time he spoke the money was burnt and the dead man's wife and children had already suffered very much . . . If I'd spoken out they would only have suffered more. He relieved his soul, poor creature, by telling me, and I took his burden on my shoulders for a little."

"I think you did right."

"But now . . ." He was thoughtful. "The wife is dead too, she died a few months ago, and the children have emigrated to Australia . . . Perhaps I could tell Joe now."

"He isn't going to like the thought of all that money burnt."

"This is one confession you have allowed me to make to you, Chloe," said John Azzopardi gratefully.

They walked on back to Dr. De Bono's house.

For a few minutes there was silence between them. Then Azzopardi spoke: "You know, Chloe, on that afternoon when we visited the Inquisitor's Palace I had such a strange feeling when we looked at the prison . . . But do you know, I realise now it wasn't caused by the prison. No. I was thinking about a man and a barrow. We'd better hurry, Chloe."

At the table Aunt Lily Louise sipped her wine (she had no palate whatsoever and did not really care for wine, but she knew that sipping from a slim glass with ringed hands can make a very elegant gesture), and turned to Coffin. He was a little replete now with food and wine and was sitting quietly. He smiled at the Baroness Castaldi dreamily; he liked a handsome woman.

"So nice for them to have another child," she said. "For Alice, particularly. Children are women's work, are they not, Inspector?" went on Lily Louise with the conviction of one who had handed over her own children to a well-trained staff and only got to know them as adults.

"Yes," agreed Coffin cautiously. In his own world it was no longer strictly true, most husbands were competent nannies; he fully expected to do some pram-pushing himself and he had no doubt whatever that

Patsy had some more menial jobs lined up for him. "Men are creeping in," he said.

"Ah, but there are some things they cannot do," said Lily Louise archly, perhaps she had sipped too much wine. "They cannot actually give birth."

"Not quite," agreed Coffin, "very nearly, but not quite."

In his society there was a keen rivalry between the young wives as to whose childbirth was the most natural and whose husband had stayed with them the longest. "Roddy was there the *whole* time," was the proudest boast. The attitude of the young husbands was noticeably less straightforward.

"I don't know how you felt about it, dear boy," said one. "But I didn't feel quite comfortable."

"Tricky position. No protocol for it."

"You can say that again. I could see the nurse didn't like having me there. She kept giving me hostile glances and telling me to move. I wouldn't have minded if I could really have helped Glenda, but she was more interested in herself by that time. I was a status symbol, that's what I was . . . And frankly, old boy," he lowered his voice, "I couldn't afford the *time*."

"It gets quicker with the later ones," said his friend.

"It seems a wicked thing to say, but there was a report I ought to have been drafting," he sighed. "There's another thing too: prejudices a man's relationship with his son from the start. I mean how's he going to feel when he hears about it later (and Glenda tells everyone) to remember you first saw him all red-faced and greasy.

It cuts at the dignity there ought to be between a man and his son. But women never see that. I believe in Artemis and the Mysteries of Diana, and all that, don't you?" he added wistfully. "That was the right way of looking at it. It's fierce magic, really, taboo, dangerous to meddle."

Coffin himself had said delicately to Patsy that he thought he was "a little too old", to which she had answered with feeling that the only person who would like it less than him would be her. For this humane and liberal attitude Coffin had been grateful.

"It's a rat race," he said aloud absently to Baroness Castaldi. She looked surprised.

"Is that what you think?"

"As a matter of fact I don't know what I think or what my wife thinks," he added, "of me or anything."

Far away in London his wife Patsy was having a conversation with her closest woman friend, another actress, and a famous one, called Venetia Stuart. She was telling a story; she told it well, she was a good actress.

"And he said to me, 'Marrying you is the most important thing I ever did in my life.' And I said, 'What? More important than being a policeman? Making a success of life?' And he answered, 'Much more' . . . And I thought, How strange you should say that when to me it seems utterly trivial compared with all the other things that shaped us first – education, ambitions, police work, my acting. And then I thought: I suppose the thing is that John really believes in the importance of human relationships and I, in the end, do not." She sounded sad.

"Do you know," said Coffin to Lily Louise Castaldi, "I really think I must have had a little too much wine. I feel a little dizzy and I fancied I heard my wife's voice."

Lily Louise poured him some coffee, and took some herself.

Sergeant Grima was summoned to the telephone; he was gone for a very short time, hardly long enough for Coffin and the Baroness to finish their coffee. When he came back he had a strange look on his face.

"Is it Green?" said De Bono quickly. "He's gone?"

"No, no, there's no more news about him; he'll probably live . . ." he paused. "They've found the Grech girl."

"Where?"

The sergeant took a deep breath. "By the roadside in the country out towards Marsa Scala. She'd been left there. Lying in the road."

"She's dead then?" The sergeant nodded silently.

"For how long?"

"Her body was still warm," said the sergeant bitterly. "Still warm."

The Last Inquisition

VIII

While the detectives were eating their dinner and pursuing, for a little while, their own lives, Rose Grech was lying supine, her eyes closed, her mouth crusted with fever, her skin dry and scaly. Her breathing was laborious and noisy. The knife she had once sharpened was on the floor beside her unwanted.

The door was wide open and she had been dragged forward into the light. But there was no longer any point in hoping that a good look at her would show she was really all right. A good look at her showed only too clearly that all was wrong.

"This girl's very ill," said the man who had brought her there and who had been her captor. There were other ways to describe him, and other terms to use of his relationship with her, but this was the way Rose had thought of him in her last conscious moments and therefore this is the best way to describe him now. But make no mistake, Rose had identified him and the place where she lay. She had guessed everything from the damp earthy smell of potatoes.

She was lying on a bed in a stone hut of the sort used to store vegetables. This resting place had made her think for a time she was in a prison. For a second she had even had a mad thought that perhaps she was shut up in a cell in the Old Inquisitor's Palace. But Rose Grech was not in a prison. She was in an ordinary shed. It was chilly and airless and usually dark. Now the door was wide open when it was too late for Rose to walk out. The knife she had sharpened and never used lay on the ground beside her. Rose was past holding a knife now.

"I didn't realise she was going to get ill like this. Why didn't you tell me how bad she was? Well, she'll have to go to hospital, that's what, or she'll die on us." He was troubled. "God knows I didn't want to harm the girl, I only wanted to keep her quiet."

"Wasn't it harming her then to hit her on the head and then lock her up here?" cried Rose Grech's sister. "Wasn't that cruel beyond anything?" She was sobbing at what she had found.

"I only wanted to stop her shouting her head off."

"Like Hector?" inquired the girl bitterly.

"She kept saying we must tell the truth. What did she know about it?"

"As much as Hector."

"Don't keep on saying that."

"That's what you said to Hector."

"You're in this just as much as anyone."

"No I am not." The girl measured out the syllables carefully. "I was asleep. And anyway I'm only fifteen. I'm not in anything. You can't threaten me. It'll all come out now when she gets to hospital. You know what they are like there. Questions. How long has she been like this? How did she get like this? *Where have you been keeping her?*" She danced back. "No, you can't hit me."

"I shan't take her to hospital then."

"You've got to. I say so. I found her where you had her hidden, and I say so." She was a dominating girl, with all the family characteristics.

"No, I shall take her to the bus-stop on the Mosta road and put her in the shelter there and leave her. Someone will find her and *they* can take her to hospital."

"Cruel."

"You can say what you like about you not being in this, but you are, you can't help it, we all are. Wouldn't it be better if it was all forgotten?"

"The police won't forget. Sergeant Grima won't."

"They would have to if they never found out any more. And who's to tell them?"

"Rose."

"She's sick; when she's well she'll think better of it too."

In spite of herself the girl was beginning to be convinced; she was only fifteen.

"Now help me with her. Wrap her coat round her and I'll get her on the road."

So Rose Grech's journey continued. It was now on its last lap. Neither of them noticed that somewhere between the hut and the Mosta road, she simply stopped breathing. Rose Grech's journey was done.

At the hospital they at once detected certain things.

"The girl has not been poisoned or attacked. She died naturally. She had measles. A bad fulminating case. Pneumonia had set in as a complication of this disease. She had been neglected."

That made one point.

"She had been lying amongst earth and potatoes. There are fragments of potato tubers in her hair and soil on her shoes and under her finger-nails."

That made a second point.

And on a label tied round her wrist someone had written: "Next of kin is Amelia Grech. Grandmother lives at Marsa Scala."

That made points three and four.

The themes were repeating themselves as in a piece of music; anger, fear, and unreason winding into their climax.

The last inquisition to be conducted in the Grech case was in full swing. An ominous word, Coffin thought, but the death penalty is never exacted in Malta. This murderer would not swing. Privately, Coffin considered that there might be another reason apart from public opinion, why this murderer would never be executed.

On this occasion only one person, Mary Colombo, was being questioned. She was pale but her eyes were dry. The time for tears was long past. This time, willy nilly, she was telling the truth.

The pattern of the questioning had been decided beforehand by the three men. Only John Azzopardi had said nothing.

"You were frightened?" asked the Inquisitor.

"Yes, I was very frightened."

"And that was why you lied? Consistently lied to us?"

"We were all frightened."

"It is you I am asking. You were threatened with violence, personal violence?"

She nodded, unable to speak.

"Was it just a threat? Or did you at any time ever actually receive violence?"

For answer Mary Colombo held out her arms. "My arms, Peter Fenech's face, Mrs. Callus . . . even Olive Feltcher has bruises."

"So. Let us recapitulate: you lied when you said you heard a noise and came down to look?"

"Yes, I lied."

"There was a noise but you did not have to come down to investigate . . . *You were there all the time?*"

"Yes, I was there inside. I was housekeeping . . ."

"This was demanded of you?"

She hesitated and he repeated the question. "Yes, it was forced labour. I did it most nights. I was scared."

"And it was as you scrubbed that night Hector was killed, you came through from the other room and saw him lying there on the floor? Already, as you thought, dead?"

"Yes," whispered Mary Colombo.

"And Carmel Grech said: help me lift him on the bed and you did so?"

"Yes. It was just before he went to work."

"The man without a name," said De Bono bitterly.

"I suppose he must have hated that anonymity and the son who was not his son."

"He's hardly appeared in the case before," said Grima ruefully.

"Except with his barrow," pointed out John Azzopardi. "He carried Rose Grech in that till he could get her into the van he borrowed."

De Bono resumed his questioning of Mary Colombo.

"And the others in the house – what did they know?"

"They knew afterwards," said the girl. "They heard the noise; they soon understood."

"I bet they did," said Coffin.

"And at this time, the boy's head was still on his body and he was not decapitated?"

"No," said Mary Colombo, rolling her eyes round in her head as if she might faint.

"And in your opinion what was the cause of his murder?"

"He was calling out, struggling and angry because his bird was dead. He said his mother had neglected it – let it starve. I don't know. It was a weak bird; I think it just died. But Hector wouldn't believe that. He was hard to control, poor Hector. Perhaps it was an accident." And now Mary Colombo did start to cry, wearily and slowly as if any more effort was beyond her.

"And the figure you saw climbing out of the ground floor window was Hector Grech himself trying to escape his beating? You saw him from the *inside*, not the outside as you previously told us?"

"Yes, yes, yes," cried Mary.

"It was the first real piece of hard truth she told us," thought John Azzopardi. "No wonder she showed a kind of relief when she told us."

But De Bono had one more question. "You all of you lied because you were frightened?"

"Yes," said Mary Colombo. "We all of us lied because we were frightened."

"Well, we were all correct about one thing," said Coffin when she had left them to sit again in the outer room, "we said that when we knew why she went down into the room to see what had happened we should know the murderer."

"But we still do not know why his head was cut off," said John Azzopardi. "Was it sheer malice?"

"I'm sure it was not," said Coffin, "but once again a fear of some sort. We shall find out."

"Poor frightened, unhappy people," said John Azzopardi compassionately. "It's as if there was a curse on the Grech family. Hector, Rose, the first husband . . ."

Nobody answered.

"The policeman on duty in St. Michael's Street overheard Amelia Grech accusing the others of poisoning her," said Grima suddenly. "Do you think that is possible?"

Coffin shook his head. "No. I don't think they've poisoned her. I've seen her. In my opinion she's had a slight stroke. Yes. She has the unsteady gait, the sleepiness, the air of weakness which mark it."

. . . . .

Rose Grech's stepfather, a stocky dark-haired man inclined to plumpness, stood before his mother-in-law, who was also his distant cousin, and tried to make her understand how he felt.

"I didn't want to hurt the girl, you see that? And after all, who would have supposed she would collapse like that?" He sounded aggrieved.

"She was locked up," observed the old woman. She was aged beyond her years because she had lost all her teeth. Over her head she wore the black tent-like erection of a faldetta. "I didn't like her being locked up but you said she must be. I don't understand. She was locked in a shed back of my own house. But I never understood why."

"Don't understand or won't understand," thought Carmel Grech. But he could hardly blame her.

"I had to do it."

He was silent.

"Don't understand. Honour thy father and thy mother, that's what we're taught," said the old lady who was genuinely bewildered.

"Rose did not honour her mother much, and as for me, I'm only her stepfather." He was not only her stepfather but a distant cousin; he had also been her own father's cousin which was why they bore the same name, Grech. "I have no child of my own." He could not keep the bitterness from his voice.

"You must pray. Go to Mosta Church," said the old lady eagerly.

"I'm not looking for a miracle."

She looked distressed.

"What a man wants is a proper home life and a family of his own. And he wants it to come without praying for it."

"You shouldn't say things like that." Naturally pious and devout herself, Carmel had shocked her.

"I do say it. You're always at it and what good has it ever done you?"

"I am happy."

"No, you're not. You're a fool if you are." He looked round the poor plain room.

"I am content."

"Ah, that's different." He looked sardonic. "You can make what you like of that, can't you? I mean you could be content in a pig-sty. Now I'm like Alfred Grima. I want things good in this world."

"Politics," said his mother-in-law, practically spitting out the words. "You'll be excommunicated."

"I suppose I shall be that anyway as things stand."

"Not if you repent – confess."

"I shan't do that."

"How you must have hated Hector," she said in sadness. "All of you. Even his own Aunt Violet. She thinks only of her own husband now."

"Well, you can't blame her. But you've got it wrong. No one hated Hector."

"Confess!"

"What, and give Alfred Grima best?" He walked to the window. "Amelia always liked Alfred Grima . . . And he liked her once. A long while ago now. Perhaps she'd have done better to marry him."

He came away from the window.

"You don't think . . . No, it couldn't be," the words stumbled on his lips, "that Hector was Alfred Grima's son?"

"The wicked, wicked things you say," she screamed at him.

The music was still playing in Mrs. Callus's room. *Tosca* is a long as well as a dramatic opera and Amelia had sat through the last scenes several times. Mrs. Callus wondered if she herself would ever be able to listen to it with pleasure again. But she might not be given the chance. Was she not an accessory after the fact of murder, sharing an almost equal guilt in the eyes of the law with the murderer? Everyone in the house, to a greater or lesser degree, had been an accessory with her. An accessory through silence.

The brilliant, voluptuous, murderous music poured over them as they sat in silence. Finally it ceased and the room was still.

Amelia Grech leaned back in her chair and pushed her hands forward in that curious gesture John Azzopardi had noticed in her.

"If only I had known sooner that such music existed . . . I'd never have had to kill him."

"I don't believe you," said Mrs. Callus bitterly.

"I would never have got so angry. This music takes the violence out of you."

"It was never necesesary to kill him, a boy like that."

"It was an accident. You could call it that. He made such a noise, shouting over the bird. I hit him."

"You raise your hand too often."

"Yes, you are frightened of me," said Amelia proudly. She raised her right arm and stared at it. "I could beat any one of you, man or woman. And I would too."

Mrs. Callus said nothing; she had reason to know this statement was true. Her own bruises burned.

"I made you all keep quiet, didn't I? You knew what Amelia could do to you."

"We were fools. We should have let them lock you up. Then you couldn't have touched any of us."

Amelia shrugged. "You should have thought of that sooner." Her face hardened. "You all hated Hector. My husband hated Hector. We were childless, he and I, *we* had no son. But there was Hector. Of course he was rough with the boy. I was the one that loved Hector so I was the right one to chastise him."

"You didn't have to kill him."

"What happens is what you have to do," said Amelia. All that she had been taught in her youth and heard in her Church seemed to have been rejected; all that she had left was this profoundly pessimistic and un-Christian attitude. She was staring forward into space.

Mrs. Callus was trembling. This was the first time Amelia had spoken of the murder in such clear terms.

"I came back from being with Olive and saw that Hector had moved from the bed where I had placed him." She turned her terrible face towards her landlady. "I had to make sure he was dead, you see, so I cut off his head. I couldn't have him moving around half-dead." Her voice dropped. "His eyes. His eyes had tears. He had been weeping." Thick tears gathered on her own cheeks, her mouth twisted and she tried to attract Mrs. Callus's attention. But Mrs. Callus had fainted.

The gramophone, set in motion by Mrs. Callus's fall, picked up again automatically and Verdi's music flooded out.

When Sergeant Grima in company with John Coffin burst open the door, the two women were both still and silent and the air was full of music.

"She's only fainted," said Sergeant Grima, raising his head from Mrs. Callus and keeping his hand on her pulse. "It's a bad one, though, we shall have to get her to a doctor, she may have had a heart attack. Turn that noise off," he added to the constable who had followed them in.

Amelia was immobilised in her chair. Only her eyes moved in her face.

"What about her?" asked Grima striding over.

"She, too, needs a doctor," said Coffin; only with difficulty could he move his gaze from that flickering, never still, hypnotic stare that fixed his own. "Perhaps unconscious hypnotism as well as brute force had been behind her domination of all these people," he reflected. The entire household had been terrorised into keeping quiet about the identity of the murderer; her husband had been forced to help; only her daughter Rose had tried to speak out, and for that she had been imprisoned in the shed on her grandmother's village house at Marsa Scala, being transported out there like a bundle of washing in the barrow and then in the van in which her stepfather distributed Amelia's work.

"She is paralysed," he said, tearing his eyes away.

Grima came and stood over her. Their eyes met. Her lips moved and her throat muscles strained with the effort to speak.

"*Alfred Grima*," she laboured out.

There was no more. What she was trying to say remained for ever unknown.

Grima stared at her and moved away.

Afterwards Coffin said to John Azzopardi, "I knew as soon as I saw her, that first day I landed in Malta, that she'd had a slight stroke. I could tell the signs. And I thought: yes, she's had an emotional shock, a great one, so all right . . . And then I thought: but perhaps she's been under a physical strain too, the strain of attacking the boy and then of cutting off his head. She's a great strong woman still. I think from that moment I knew she could be and probably was guilty. I told your cousin so."

Dr. De Bono had taken John Coffin to lunch in his club to say good-bye.

"Have the fish," he had recommended, pouring from a carafe of wine. "It's good on Wednesday."

"Good always," mumbled Coffin, through a mouthful of crusty bread. "I'm going to miss this bread."

"I am glad you will take some happy memories of us away."

Coffin opened his eyes wide. "I shall take plenty. Everything has been good."

"But the case itself!" De Bono opened his eyes wide.

"That was a job and we did it. Did it well too. I congratulate you and Grima."

"I would not like you to think we have many people like Amelia Grech."

"I don't condemn Amelia Grech; I feel a lot of understanding and pity for her." Coffin drank some wine. He knew himself that family relationships can be destructive. Thinking of Patsy, he unobtrusively crossed his fingers. "Anyway, I am thinking more of my friends here." He met De Bono's eyes and smiled. "You must let me give you a return match."

"I don't think I'd be equal to your London criminals," said De Bono, leaning back to receive his fish which the waiter placed proudly before him.

"I believe you always suspected Amelia Grech."

"Suspected is a hard word." De Bono neatly filletted his fish and called for a clean plate to put the bones on. "She *troubled* me. Yes, from the beginning I was troubled by Amelia Grech."

"This was before you sent for me?"

"It was the reason I sent for you." De Bono looked apologetic. "I am afraid I kept something from you and my cousin Azzopardi."

Coffin smiled. "Go on."

"I pretended to him that I sent for you because of

political stresses. There may have been a little element of that, not much. No. I knew that once in the past Alfred Grima had – well, shall we say, courted Amelia."

"He had a feeling for her," nodded Coffin. "I noticed that. So did Azzopardi. But I couldn't tell whether he liked or disliked her. He's a bit of an enigma, your Alfred."

"A strong man," acknowledged Joe De Bono, "but an honest one. Of course all this friendship with Amelia was long, long past and all I knew was gossip, nothing of my own knowledge, you understand."

"So that was where I came in," said Coffin. He was thinking that if the gossips had said Hector Grech was Alfred's son then Dr. De Bono had done well to call in an outsider. But to have acted with such discretion that nothing had been said openly and nothing dragged out even now had been most skilful. Grima's career could have been marred. As it was, not even his pride had been damaged. Coffin looked at De Bono, placidly eating his fish, with affectionate respect.

"You see, I couldn't afford to let Grima know I had heard the gossip," went on De Bono. "I like him, I trust him, but sometimes I think he hardly believes it."

"He is a little bit wary of the good things of life," agreed Coffin, who was inclined to be the same himself. "Policemen get that way."

"The case really began long before the boy was killed. You might call that the end and not the beginning."

"Yes, we're always called in too late, more like undertakers than doctors to society. We ought to be crime preventors not crime detectors, and we *could* be given half a chance."

"I am a lawyer, not a policeman like you," corrected De Bono. "But I agree with you. The case started when the dissatisfaction that Amelia Grech and her husband Carmel felt with each other boiled over into quarrels. One pointless quarrel after the other. The neighbours knew."

"They had cause to do," pointed out Coffin, "with Amelia using her strength to intimidate them."

"It progressed," said De Bono, reliving the history of the crime. "From the first quarrel it went on, at first only *about* the boy Hector, and then involving him, and finally *killing* him. A terrible and almost inevitable progression."

"The dead bird," began Coffin.

"The dead bird was the occasion, an excuse, could only be an excuse," went on De Bono with conviction, "for the ultimate act of violence. Oh, no doubt Amelia neglected the bird until it died, possibly she even killed it with her great clumsy hands, and no doubt Hector showed anger that provoked her. But by that time she must have wanted to kill. And it was going to be either Hector or her husband. Her husband was out – so," he shrugged.

Coffin considered. "No. I don't accept that. I see this boy's murder as an arbitrary act of violence that need never have happened, almost an accident. Amelia was ill – yes, to that extent some explosive act was perhaps inevitable, but it might just as easily have been a broken chair or window." He added: "This seems to me the terrible tragedy of it all."

There was a moment's silence. Then De Bono took up his knife and fork again.

"It comes to the same thing in the end: the boy was killed." He began to eat his fish again. "And later his mother cut off his head; that to *me* is the most terrible tragedy of all.

"I understand now why she cut off his head – it was not just a casual act of violence. He was knocked down by her in the kitchen, she carried him through to the bedroom and laid him on the bed. Then she went down to Olive's to make her imbecile attempt at an alibi. But he wasn't dead. Dying but not dead. People with head injuries can do strange things. Between her going out and her coming in the boy moved, and when she came home she saw this and was terrified."

"She cut off his head to make sure he was quite dead. Terrible in its simplicity, isn't it? And, of course, as the post-mortem showed, he *was* dead by that time."

The waiter came forward with an elaborate pale pink pudding. De Bono refused it and offered his guest cheese and fruit. "An Arabic pudding – too sweet for you."

"Is it?" Coffin looked at it wistfully, his mouth watered, but he understood he must live up to his reputation of a tough London policeman. His mind was still full of the story of Amelia Grech and her family.

"The Grech daughters saw the original quarrel?"

"Of course. So did Mary Colombo. The rest of the house heard. They did not know then that Hector was dead. The girls went to bed; the house became quiet."

"I suppose I ought not to be amazed at the endless capacity for people keeping quiet and saying nothing," said Coffin. "They were frightened, of course."

"Rose Grech did want to speak out, poor child," De Bono reminded him. "But was locked up by her stepfather to prevent her doing so."

"What will happen to the girls now?"

"They are going to live with the grandmother and their stepfather will provide for them. Oddly enough they are all still fond of each other."

"I think you are affectionate people here," said Coffin. "Capable of deep affections."

De Bono nodded. "I love my wife. I love Alice. And *you* like me for admitting it out loud."

"Yes."

"That's because you are English," said De Bono, not without amusement. "But you would not say it out loud yourself, would you?"

"Yes, I would," said Coffin. "Listen to me. I love my wife." But he could not manage to put much conviction into this undeniably true statement.

He met De Bono's eyes and the two men burst into laughter.

Coffin remembered and was warmed by the laughter as he returned to the present and John Azzopardi.

The sun was out in a clear blue sky. The plane which would carry Coffin back to London was already waiting. It was raining in London.

"I've liked it here," he said. "I'm glad to have met Dr. De Bono. A good man. Perhaps a great one."

"Joe?" Azzopardi was surprised.

"Yes. Not the stuff that martyrs are made of perhaps, but he's something better than that," said Coffin, his enthusiasm kindling, "he's the sort that stops martyrs being necessary. Yes, the salt of the earth."

Azzopardi digested this; Coffin was giving him a new view of his cousin, and indirectly of his island itself. "I shall have to take us more seriously," he thought with the surprise of a goldfish which thought it had outgrown its bowl but finds other people don't think so.

"I'm fond of Joe, of course. He's my cousin, in some remote degree."

"They're all your cousins."

"We are a family people," said John Azzopardi seriously. "We set great store by the family."

"So you do," agreed Coffin, wondering if his friend saw the irony of the Grech family tragedy. Perhaps a looser family bond there and two deaths would have been averted. But you couldn't tell. He sighed.

"And your own family," inquired Azzopardi delicately. "Your wife. You are happy?" He had seen enough of his friend at home to know there was a question.

"Patsy? Oh yes," replied Coffin, thinking he could hardly explain the intricacies of an Anglo-Saxon marriage to his friend. "You look after your friend Chloe, a nice, reliable girl."

"I will," said Azzopardi, getting another shock. He had never thought of Chloe as reliable, but he saw now she certainly was. He held out his hand in farewell. "They're calling your name. You'd better go now before you re-think my whole island for me."

"Give my love to Grima," called Coffin over his shoulder.

On the plane he found himself sitting opposite his friend of the journey out.

"I'm off to Sicily," said the young man, taking off his dark spectacles and calling for brandy. "They've got a Weeping Madonna there. I shall do a film about her."

"I expect she's got plenty to weep about."

"I hope she weeps for me. I've never seen a Weeping Madonna before."

"I think I just left one behind," said Coffin under his breath. Or was that blasphemy? He turned his face for a last look in good-bye towards the golden island with its proud and lovable people.

If you have enjoyed this book, you might wish to join the Walker British Mystery Society.

For information, please send a postcard or letter to:

Paperback Mystery Editor

Walker & Company
720 Fifth Avenue
New York, NY 10019